"Why won't you tell me what you are hiding?"

Something inside her snapped. "At least I've given you my real name," Laura said angrily. "I'm not using a false identity. What are you hiding, Charles?"

Charles paled. "How long have you known?"

"So you don't deny it." Against all logic Laura had been cherishing the hope that there was a simple explanation, that Charles had not willfully deceived her.

"Looks as though we both have something to hide." Charles's voice was raw with suppressed emotion. "So what are we going to do now? Kiss each other goodbye and say thanks for the nice affair? Was it just that for you, Laura?"

She wanted to throw his question back at him. Had it just been a passing interlude for him—until he discovered her good fortune?

SANDRA FIELD, once a biology technician, also writes full-time under the pen names of Jocelyn Haley and Jan MacLean. She lives with her son in a rustic farmhouse in Canada's Maritimes, which she often uses as a setting for her books. She loves the independent life-style she has as a writer. She's her own boss, sets her own hours, and, increasingly there are travel opportunities.

Books by Sandra Field

These books may be available at your local bookseller.

Don't miss any of our special offers. Write to us at the following address for information on our newest releases.

Harlequin Reader Service
901 Fuhrmann Blvd., P.O. Box 1397, Buffalo, NY 14240
Canadian address: P.O. Box 2800, Postal Station A,
5170 Yonge St., Willowdale, Ont. M2N 6J3

SANDRA FIELD

one in a million

Harlequin Books

TORONTO • NEW YORK • LONDON
AMSTERDAM • PARIS • SYDNEY • HAMBURG
STOCKHOLM • ATHENS • TOKYO • MILAN

Harlequin Presents first edition August 1986
ISBN 0-373-10905-9

Original hardcover edition published in 1986
by Mills & Boon Limited

PROLOGUE

THREE gulls were squabbling on the beach over a scrap of garbage cast up by the tide. But as the man appeared on the ridge of shale, by a common signal the gulls took to the air in a heavy beat of wings.

The man stood still, watching the birds wheel over the water: creatures of another world, tinted gold by the early morning sun. He would have liked them to stay and share with him the silver-grey crescent of smooth sand, the gentle lap of the waves, the pale splendour of the sun. But they had gone. He was alone on the beach.

He began jogging down the sand.

He was used to being alone, although more often than not in his earlier years it had been an aloneness of the spirit rather than the body; because of his father there had always been people around, people paid to look after him or people who wanted something from him. The net result had been to drive him even deeper into himself and his own resources. During the past few months, in the slums of Bombay and the mountains of Nepal, he had needed those resources and been glad of them and had brought back with him a quiet inner pride at his own survival. But he had brought back his loneliness as well, and with it a scarcely articulated longing for someone who would share the beach with him . . . a woman.

He had no clear picture of her in his mind. He only knew that together they would laugh and talk and frolic in the waves; and then they would go back to the cottage, where she would banish the emptiness of his bed and the loneliness in his heart . . .

He had reached the end of the strip of sand and the promontory of grey rock that thrust against the sea. Turning, he ran back the way he had come, increasing his pace until a sheen of sweat covered his naked torso. She was an illusion, this unknown woman who would accept him for himself. His reason told him so. And to prove him right the sunlit beach remained mockingly empty.

CHAPTER ONE

WHEN Jane walked into the kitchen, she found Laura seated at the kitchen table, her head buried in her hands. She was sobbing as if her heart would break.

'Laura! What's the matter?'

Laura raised a tear-drenched face. 'Oh ... J-Jane,' she hiccupped. 'I—I didn't hear you come in.'

'I knocked, but no one answered.' Patiently Jane repeated her question. 'Laura dear, what's the matter?'

'It's Bart,' Laura wailed. 'He's—he's proposed.' A horrendous sob tore at her throat.

Jane pulled out a chair and sat down at the round oak table. It was covered with an embroidered tablecloth across which the evening sun streamed, gold and warm. Laura's cap of short, dark hair gleamed in the sun, which, impartially, also fell on her reddened eyes and pink-tipped nose. Said Jane in a neutral voice, 'Aren't you happy that he's proposed? You've been in love with him for years.'

'But why did he have to wait until now? Why couldn't he have proposed before he went away?'

'You mean, before you won the money,' Jane corrected her gently, her mild blue eyes fastened on Laura's distraught face in mingled affection and concern.

'That's right!' Laura pulled a bedraggled tissue from her pocket, looked at it dubiously and scrubbed at her eyes, a move which did not noticeably improve her appearance. 'Now I'll never know, will I? Whether he proposed because he loves me or because I won a million dollars.' The tears overflowed again from her dark brown eyes. 'Jane, it's a dreadful thing to say but there are times I wish I'd never won that wretched money. Everything's changed!'

7

'Has Darren been at you again?'

'Oh, yes. Day in and day out. Then today I met the chairman of the school board downtown and they want me to set up a scholarship fund. Yesterday it was the hospital board. Even the minister is after me—he thinks I should pay for painting the church. Oh, he didn't come right out and say it in so many words, but I got the message. I had two 'phone calls this afternoon from people I'd never heard of, and five letters asking for money.' A wry smile pulled at her mouth. 'Not asking. Demanding. And a sixth letter, which was merely obscene.'

Jane sat up straight, so that the sun touched her greying hair and her pleasant, forty-year-old face. She had been Laura's friend for four years, ever since Laura had arrived in this rambling, old-fashioned house to look after her brother's three children, Darren, Keith and Sue-Ann. Now Jane said decisively, 'It's time you got away from here for a while.'

'What will that solve? I'll only have to come back.'

'You're losing your sense of perspective. Think of all the good things you'll be able to do with that money. You can pay for the kids' education and your own as well, you can buy yourself a house in Toronto next year if you want to, and——'

'And I can paint the church,' Laura finished gloomily.

Jane laughed. 'You can paint a thousand churches if that's what turns you on. Don't keep me in suspense any longer, Laura—what did you tell Bart? Yes or no?'

'Neither.' Restlessly Laura got up from the table and went to stand by the window over the sink, her back to Jane. 'I pulled the Victorian maiden trick and said oh Bart, this is so sudden.' She thrust her hands into the pockets of her jeans. 'So sudden—ha! We've been dating each other for three years.' She suddenly turned to face her friend, genuine misery dragging at her mouth. 'He says he loves me, that he wants to marry me as soon as possible, that we've waited long enough. I—I

wish I believed him. Oh God, how I wish I believed him
... *why* couldn't he have proposed a month ago?'

Jane said calmly, 'You think he proposed because
you won the lottery.'

Staring down at the linoleum on the floor, Laura
muttered, 'Yes. I guess I do.'

Jane was not overly fond of Bart but she wanted very
badly to be fair. 'He was away from you for over a
month, Laura, on that family law course in Montreal.
Maybe he realised how he felt about you while he was
away. Absence makes the heart grow fonder, or so they
say.'

'Maybe.' But Laura did not sound convinced and her
shoulders had a disconsolate droop.

'If you married him, would you still be able to go to
medical school?'

'Oh, yes. He said he could start up a law practice in
Halifax so I could go to Dalhousie. Once Sue-Ann's
finished at school next summer.'

'He's being very accommodating. After all, he's lived
here all his life and he's the town's only lawyer. He'd be
leaving quite a bit behind.'

Laura said bitterly, 'A million dollars is a lot of
money.'

Jane bit her lip. 'You know, I meant what I said—
you should go away for a while. School finishes next
week. There's no reason why you couldn't take off for
three or four weeks. Why don't you book a flight to
Toronto, stay in a nice hotel, go shopping——'

'No!'

'You have a positive paranoia about Toronto,' Jane
said crossly. 'I know you still miss it, and I'm sure some
days you're counting the hours until you can get back
there. But that's no reason why you shouldn't visit it.'

With the ease of long friendship Laura said, 'Stop
nagging, Jane. I'm not going to Toronto.'

Jane's face brightened. 'I know—you can go to Cape
Breton. I had a——'

'I don't want to go anywhere!'

'Yes, you do. You need to get away from Darren and Keith and Sue-Ann and all their friends and their rock music and your job and the 'phone calls and the letters and—and even the unpainted church. Because I know darn well that every time you walk down Main Street and see the paint peeling on the steeple you'll feel guilty.'

'You know me too well.'

'An over-sized sense of duty,' Jane remarked. 'That's you. For which, by the way, I commend you. I know the last four years haven't been easy. Why don't you put the kettle on and make me a cup of tea while I tell you all the reasons you should go to Cape Breton next week.'

Laura crossed the room and picked up the aluminium kettle from the stove. The kitchen, large enough for the heavy oak table and chairs to be in proportion, was wallpapered in a cheerful design of brightly coloured fruits and vegetables, the surface clutter on the beige countertop giving the room a lived-in look. The window overlooked a sixty-acre apple orchard. The front of the house faced the main street of the little town of Grantham, nestled between the North and South mountains of Nova Scotia's Annapolis Valley. Laura had lived in this house, her dead brother's, for four years, had grown to appreciate the serenity of her surroundings and the slow pace of life, and had never once felt as though she belonged in Grantham or would ever belong.

Now she splashed cold water on her face and dabbed it dry on a towel before filling the kettle. 'I detest weeping females,' she said. 'Sorry.'

'We're all allowed a good cry once in a while ... Bart's been very important to you, hasn't he?'

'Yes.' Laura smiled affectionately at Jane. 'The two of you have kept me sane the past few years. I suppose I saw Bart as someone who was able to get out of Grantham and get an education—so I knew it could be done, that I wouldn't be stuck here forever. And you have to admit he's very good-looking.'

'With charm to burn,' Jane said agreeably. 'It would have been better, I think, had you had more choice. He is just about the only eligible bachelor in town.'

'I hate myself for doubting him!' Laura blurted. 'What a dreadful thing to do—suspect him of asking to marry me just because I won a lot of money. But I do doubt him. I must. Or else I'd have said yes. Heaven knows, I've imagined him proposing often enough. Trouble is, in my fantasies I melted into his arms and we lived happily ever after.'

'In Grantham?' Jane said drily.

'Fantasies don't have to be too specific,' Laura retorted, a glint of laughter in her eyes for the first time since Jane had arrived.

Purposely Jane changed the subject. 'My sister has a cottage near the mouth of the Mira River. Right on the ocean, very pretty and peaceful. I had a letter from her today saying it would be empty for all of July. It's fate, Laura. Why don't you go there for a month? It'll give you time to decide what you want to do with all that money, it will give you a break from the kids, and you can make up your mind whether or not you'll marry Bart.'

'No noisy teenagers,' said Laura dreamily.

'No rock music.'

'Keep talking. You're tempting me . . .'

Jane ticked off her fingers. 'No three meals a day, no washing or ironing or cleaning, no job at the hospital.'

'At the risk of sounding totally negative I do hate that job.'

'So you should, it's miles below your capabilities. Just think, Laura—a sand beach, sunshine, the ripple of the waves . . .'

'I could take my books and study for the medical admissions tests.'

'You could leave them at home and do nothing for a change! Wouldn't hurt you a bit. It's a very private place, only one other cottage on the peninsula—do go. I'll keep an eye on the home front for you.'

The kettle began to boil. Laura made the tea, allowing her mind's eye to dwell on the solitude of a sunlit beach hundreds of miles to the east. She would like to get away. Too much had happened in the last month; her life had changed too drastically for her to have come to terms with it. Bart was only part of the problem ... although a very real part. Thinking out loud, she said slowly, 'Money changes everything. I don't feel accepted as myself anymore since I won the lottery. I don't mean you and Dave, Jane, don't get me wrong. Or Sue-Ann and Keith. But almost everyone else seems to want something from me. It's a horrible feeling.'

'A million dollars is an awful lot of money. It's sort of a magical number, isn't it? A million dollars ... everyone's dream.'

'Trust me to win it with the only lottery ticket I ever bought in my life. I only got it for a joke.'

'And the joke didn't backfire,' Jane said stoutly. 'You're going to go away for a while to a place where no one will know you won all that money and you're going to think of all the good things it will do for you, and you'll come home rested and relaxed and able to deal with a dozen Barts.'

'It would be nice to be anonymous for a while.' Laura's eyes were wistful. 'Bart's proposal has taught me one thing—unless I'm anonymous, I'll always wonder if someone's falling in love with me for myself or for my money. That's a dreadful thought, isn't it?'

Said Jane with unwitting and total inaccuracy, 'I don't think the problem will arise at the cottage, love. When I said peace and quiet, I meant it.'

'Just as well,' Laura responded lightly. 'I am in love with Bart, after all.'

'Are you, Laura? Are you really? Or do you think it's simply that he's the only suitable man around?'

'Of course I am! Why else do you think I'm so upset that he hasn't proposed to me until now? If I didn't love him, I wouldn't care.'

'Well, maybe. Although I've always thought you're much too pretty and bright to be buried in a little place like Grantham. I'm going to be very direct and say don't marry Bart unless you're absolutely sure of your feelings. Promise?'

'I suppose so.' Laura gave Jane a troubled frown. 'I thought I was the one with doubts, not you.'

Jane said obliquely, 'When I met Dave I knew right away that he was the man I was going to marry. No doubts whatsoever.'

Dave, Jane's husband and the town pharmacist, was short, balding and portly; even twenty years ago Laura wondered how he could have been seen as a figure of romance. Yet the bond between him and Jane was real and viable, nothing to be laughed at or scorned in these days of dissolving marriages. She said with more conviction, 'I do promise I won't marry Bart unless I'm sure he's as right for me as Dave is for you.'

'Good. Why don't you pour the tea? You know I don't like it too strong.'

Laura was peering into the biscuit tins, both of which were empty. 'You're not going to be tempted off your diet, anyway. Whenever Keith's unhappy, he eats.'

Keith, now nineteen years old, was the younger of Laura's two nephews. His first year at university, majoring in commerce, had not been an outstanding success.

Jane stirred her tea. 'Hasn't he recovered from the shock of flunking two out of five of his courses yet?'

'He wants to study music instead,' Laura said.

'That's a switch! Voice?' Laura nodded. 'You don't look very happy about it.'

'His father always wanted him to take commerce and go into banking.'

'His father's dead, Laura. Dead for four years. Keith can't be bound by the expectations of someone who's no longer here. You know yourself your brother James tended to favour Keith over the other two children because he was so clever at mathematics. Keith was the heir apparent. Keith would become a stockbroker or an investment counsellor or at the very least the manager of a city bank. James never had any use for Darren or Sue-Ann, Darren because he didn't do well at school, Sue-Ann because she was only a girl.'

Laura raised a quizzical brow. 'You're being very forthright.'

'You mean I shouldn't speak ill of the dead? James had lots of good qualities but sensitivity to his children was not among them.'

'You're right, I know ... but I guess I've tried to steer Keith away from music just the same. Thought I should follow James's wishes. James was always against Keith's singing.'

'Keith's much like you, bright and ambitious. Just because James was perfectly satisfied being a bank manager doesn't mean Keith would be. Besides, you can afford to pay for his music lessons now, can't you?'

'I can, yes.' Distractedly Laura ran her fingers through her close-cropped hair. 'Sorry, Jane, I seem to be down in the dumps today.'

'You need a holiday. Will you have trouble getting time off at the hospital?'

'None whatsoever,' Laura said wryly. 'It's already been suggested to me—ever so politely—that as the winner of all that money I should quit my job at the hospital and allow someone more needy to have it. They put the touch on me for a donation to the equipment fund, too.'

'You didn't like the job, Laura.'

'No, I didn't. But it did get me out of the house.'

Jane leaned forward, resting her hand on Laura's wrist. 'A year from now Sue-Ann will be graduating from high school and you'll be free, Laura—free. You'll be able to go back to Toronto and pick up your life where you left it.' Jane, more than anyone else in Grantham, had sensed the cost to Laura of the guardianship of James's three children. At the age of twenty-one Laura had graduated from the University of

Toronto with honours in biochemistry and had been accepted into the highly regarded medical programme there. Then James, choleric, red-faced James, had died of a heart attack, leaving Darren, Keith and Sue-Ann as orphans, for their mother had died three years earlier of cancer. Their mother's relatives all lived in Saskatchewan and evinced no interest in taking on three children; Laura's parents were too old; and Laura was James's only sister. So she had come to Grantham to assess the situation and in Grantham she had stayed.

'Even if I married Bart,' Laura murmured, 'I'd still be able to go to medical school.'

'Of course you would.'

Footsteps clattered across the back porch and a door slammed. The kitchen door burst open as Sue-Ann rushed into the room. 'Hi, Jane! Laura, guess what?'

'Steven's asked you to the formal dance,' Laura said immediately. Her niece had been moping over Steven Carson for the past three weeks.

'However did you guess? Isn't it *wonderful*?' Sue-Ann plunked her books on the table and whirled around the room, a beatific smile on her pretty, heart-shaped face, her dark hair swinging. 'He's so gorgeous, I'm madly in love with him.' She added smugly, 'So are most of the other girls in my class. But I'm the one he's asked to the dance. Oh, Laura, do you think I could get a new dress?'

One of Sue-Ann's nicest traits was her complete lack of avarice. She was a sweet-tempered child, unmarked by Laura's unexpected change in fortune: that Laura could buy a whole dress shop would never occur to Sue-Ann. 'I should think we could manage a new dress,' Laura rejoined. 'We could go shopping in Halifax on the weekend if you want to.'

'Fabulous!' Sue-Ann gave Laura a hug, waltzed over to the cookie jar, added without venom, 'That pig of a Keith,' and with a wave of her scarlet-nailed fingers vanished into the hall.

'No problems with Sue-Ann,' Jane remarked.

'Never. All I have to do is keep track of who she's in love with. Which isn't always easy, mind you.'

Jane had finished her tea. 'I'd better go. I told Dave I'd total up the cash at nine-thirty when the chemists closes. I'll call my sister and tell her you'll be at the cottage, and I'll find my key. All you'll have to do is pack your clothes. Everything else is there, and there's a store where you can buy groceries.'

'Jane, I haven't really decided to go.'

'I've decided for you.' Jane pulled on her light summer jacket and blew Laura a kiss. 'Don't let Darren talk you out of it.'

After Jane had gone, Laura sat at the kitchen table, her hands cupped around her mug. Sue-Ann had put a record on the stereo in the living room; over a bass that throbbed like a primitive heartbeat the vocalist screamed out his anger in a high-pitched, androgynous wail. Incongruous music for Sue-Ann, the gentlest of girls. Ever since she was five Sue-Ann had wanted to be a nurse. She was a volunteer at the small local hospital and a straight A student in high school, she had a wide circle of friends, she loved sports and boys. She would be an excellent nurse, compassionate yet firm. Any of Laura's attempts to undermine James's chauvinism and to suggest that medical school was just as much an option for women as for men had met with a firm refusal. 'Doctors do the decision-making, I know. But nurses look after the patients. The type of care they give can make an immense difference to a patient's well-being and morale. I want to be a nurse, Laura—that's where the action is.' So Laura had desisted, admiring the depth of Sue-Ann's dedication. No, there had never been any problems with Sue-Ann.

As she glanced around the kitchen she couldn't help remembering the scene four summers ago. James had died while Laura was writing her final exams for her bachelor's degree, so she had been unable to attend the funeral. She had arrived in Grantham a week later on the evening bus from Halifax and had gone straight to the house. All three children were in the kitchen, lined up against the counter. *Backs to the wall*, Laura had thought with a touch of humour she had decided not to share. Darren, sixteen, was stony-eyed with resentment; Keith, a year younger, was reserving judgment, his thin, intelligent face watchful. Sue-Ann had smiled, a shy, tentative smile for the aunt she had met only three times in her life. 'You're not going to take us away from here, are you?' she had said. 'We don't want to go to Toronto. We want to stay in Grantham.'

Laura sighed. They had all stayed in Grantham, all four of them ... what else was to be done? And although Darren had remained resentful, Keith had eventually warmed to her, while Sue-Ann had been her friend from the beginning. She poured herself another cup of tea and went in search of her writing paper, wincing at the cacophony from the living room.

She was sitting at the kitchen table writing her weekly letter to her parents when Keith came home an hour later, his red hair ruffled, his face incandescent with excitement. 'Remember I told you I'd sent some tapes to Toronto?' he exclaimed. 'I've got two auditions, Laura—two! One's with Besicaglia—he's the best teacher in Canada. Laura, if you'll lend me the money for my fare, I'll pay you back at the end of the month, that's when I get my first pay cheque.'

Carefully Laura laid down her pen. 'What if you're accepted? Will you give up the commerce programme?'

Keith pulled out a chair and sat down across from her. 'Yes. I'll have to. I know Dad wanted me to be a bank manager like him, but I'd die shut up in an office. I want to sing, Laura. I want to be the best tenor in Canada. And if Besicaglia takes me on, there's a chance I will be. Providing I work my guts out and don't think about anything else for the next ten years.'

How could she argue, she who was as burningly ambitious as he? Of James's three children Keith was the one most like herself; divorced from his singing, he would suffer a frustration as intense as hers had been ever since she had left Toronto. She had been cut off from the life she had loved. The last thing she could do was lock Keith in a similar prison. Jane was right. Laura could not force a dead father's expectations on a living son. 'I'll lend you the money,' she said. 'When will you go?'

Only as he let out his breath in a long sigh of relief did Laura realise Keith had been anticipating refusal. 'In three weeks.'

'I'll be away,' she said realising that somehow the decision to go away had been made. 'But you must 'phone me as soon as you know the results.'

Keith winked. 'Taking off with Bart?'

'No,' she replied with immense dignity. 'I'm going to Jane's sister's cottage in Cape Breton. Alone.'

'Doesn't sound like much fun to me.' His brow wrinkled. 'Need to get away from the the fuss about the money?' Keith could be astonishingly perceptive even when caught up in his own concerns.

'Hit the nail on the head.'

'Have a good time. Does that mean we're to be subjected to the marvels of Sue-Ann's cooking?'

Laura said with the incredulous smile that the thought of her bank balance could still produce, 'We'll get a housekeeper, I can afford it. That way I won't have to worry about you.'

'You worry too much, darling Laura,' he responded with the sensitivity that underlay his quicksilver personality; Keith, Laura had long ago decided, would make some woman a wonderful husband. 'Don't let Darren dump a guilt trip on you, will you? Just because you're taking a well-earned holiday.'

'I'll try not to,' she responded drily. 'Want anything to eat?'

'Yeah ... I'm starving. Besicaglia, Laura ... Besicaglia! I can't believe it!'

She smiled at him, unable to resist his excitement. 'I made doughnuts, and hid them under the counter,' she said primly. 'But I guess Besicaglia calls for a celebration. Just leave a couple for Darren, will you?'

Darren came home half an hour later, his big frame filling the doorway. At six-feet-one he towered over the rest of the family. He had broad cheekbones, thick, springing black hair, and shoulders like a football player; he was as different from Keith—and from James—as could be imagined.

Knowing he would not speak first, Laura said clearly, 'Hello, Darren.' He was bending to unlace his workboots and grunted a reply. 'How did work go today?' Since March he had been doing odd jobs at a local vineyard.

'Got laid off until the harvest.'

He was watching for her reaction, no doubt hoping she would be upset. She said casually, 'That's too bad. But it will work out well in one way. I want to go away for three or four weeks and——'

'Taking a world cruise?' he drawled. 'Nice that you can afford it.'

'Isn't it?' she responded coolly. 'While I hate to disappoint you, I'm only going as far as Cape Breton. To Jane's sister's cottage.'

'Still busy denying you won all that money?'

Darren had always had the knack of getting under her skin. She gave him a considering look, weighing her reply, wishing not for the first time that he was not quite so large. 'Taking time to plan my strategy, Darren.'

'With Keith in a dither about an operatic career and Sue-Ann throwing herself at Steve Carson, I would hardly have thought it was a good time for you to disappear. You are, after all, our legal guardian.'

No guilt trips . . . 'You've never forgiven me for that, have you?'

His lashes flickered, for she was not usually so direct. 'The subject bores me.'

Laura gave an unbelieving snort of laughter. 'Tell me another one,' she said. 'You resented me from the moment I walked in that door.' And so he had. At sixteen Darren had considered himself old enough to look after his younger brother and sister without her help, and had done his best ever since to make life unpleasant enough for her that she would leave. But Laura had stayed. She had tried to be understanding, knowing Darren must be missing his mother as well as his father, realising that she herself was only five years older than he and as such suspect. But her attempts at conciliation had never been reciprocated, and Darren disliked her as much now as he had then.

He had crossed the kitchen. 'Anything to eat?'

'Doughnuts in the tin in the left-hand cupboard. Darren, I'll be gone for most of July. You'll keep an eye on Keith and Sue-Ann, won't you? I'll hire a housekeeper, but that's not quite the same as having a family member around.'

Too late she saw that she had left herself wide open. 'It's not, is it?' he said unpleasantly. 'Which is why I'm surprised you're going. Are you taking the car?'

'Yes. Of course.'

'So what am I supposed to use?' His fists were clenched at his sides, his always volatile temper rising. 'You could buy a second car without even noticing now that you've got all that money. But you won't do that, will you? You won't do anything that would help me out!'

'Darren, that's not true! But I have to have time to think out how I'm going to handle the money. I've only had it for two weeks! I don't want to make any hasty decisions—and that includes buying a second car.' Her brown eyes were sparked with anger, and had he but seen it, with an intense honesty. 'It's nothing personal against you, please believe me.'

'Will you pay for Keith to go to Toronto?'

'I'm going to lend him his airfare.'

'Then lend me the money for a car.'

'That's hardly the same thing. One's a couple of hundred dollars, the other's several thousand. Darren, I promise I'll think about a second car. But I need time, don't you understand? Everyone I meet is after me for money—I've got to get away and think it all out!'

As he swung around he knocked the lid of the doughnut tin off the counter; he had always been clumsy, ever since a child, another trait deplored by his neat-fingered father. 'So go away,' he growled. 'But don't expect me to nursemaid Keith and Sue-Ann.'

Laura bit back a number of retorts. 'Will you be able to get another job over the summer?'

He shrugged. 'Dunno. Probably.' Holding a plateload of doughnuts and a glass of juice he left the room.

Childishly Laura pulled a face after him, then got herself one of the few remaining doughnuts. She was probably being ridiculous not to buy a second car; the amount of money it would represent was a drop in the bucket. But she had had too many years of scrimping and saving to lose her innate caution about money matters overnight. And maybe at some deep level she didn't quite believe that the money was real.

Munching the doughnut thoughtfully, she realised that Darren's opposition had hardened rather than weakened her resolve to go away. Jane had put her finger on a very real problem: Laura did need space. Not only to think about the money, but also to sort out her feelings about Bart and his over-hasty proposal.

The final touch was added the following morning when Laura was walking down Main Street towards the hospital where she worked part time as a laboratory assistant.

She had her resignation in the pocket of her uniform; because she was part time, she only had to give a week's notice. Her eyes winced away from the church steeple where, indeed, the paint was blistered and cracked, and met instead the ingenuous blue eyes of Bart's mother, who was approaching her on the pavement. 'Laura! How nice to see you, dear.' She gave a conspiratorial glance around her and lowered her voice. 'Have you set a wedding date yet, dear? I was so happy when Bart told me he'd asked you to marry him—such a good

match. I know you'll be very happy. Although I'm sure
once you've thought about it you won't expect Bart to
leave here and move to Halifax, will you, dear? Once
you're happily married,' she gave a girlish giggle, 'and
with the patter of little feet in the house, you won't
want to go to medical school, I know. I told Bart I was
sure you wouldn't.'

Laura counted to ten, tried to swallow the knot of
fury in her throat and said, 'There are a great many
decisions to be made in the next few weeks, Mrs
Manning, including whether or not I will accept Bart's
proposal.'

The blue eyes blinked incredulously, for how could
any woman turn down her handsome, charming son?
'You'd be very foolish not to accept him,' said Mrs
Manning severely.

'You may be right.' The fault was not with Mrs
Manning, Laura knew, who was a well-meaning if
foolish woman. The fault was with Bart for daring to
tell his mother that she, Laura, had agreed to marry
him. Laura patted the other woman on the arm. 'I'm
sure everything will work out. Now I've got to run or
I'm going to be late for work.'

As she hurried down the pavement, which was
shaded by tall, doomed elm trees, she found herself
thinking with perfect coherence: I'm going away next
week. I'm going to get out of Grantham. Away from
the kids and Bart and Mrs Manning. And the wretched
church steeple. I'm going to lie in the sun and rejoice in
the solitude.

She had no idea it would not work out that way.
Solitude, or so she thought, was what she wanted. And
solitude was what the cottage in Cape Breton would
provide.

CHAPTER TWO

THE restaurant was small but brightly lit. 'Annie's Home-Cooked Meals' it announced on a red-and-white sign over the door. In tribute to Annie's cooking, two big transport trucks were parked outside; Laura had long known that truckers were fussy about their meals. She parked beside a moving van, picked up her shoulder bag and locked the car.

It was evening and very peaceful, the sky merging from gold to a pale, eggshell blue high above the jagged black line of trees. A child's voice rose and fell in the garden of a nearby house where the lights shone yellow in the dusk, while through the trees Laura could glimpse the steel-grey stillness of the sea. She stretched her legs, for it had been a long drive. A hundred miles back she had had to stop at a garage to have the fan belt replaced, so she was later than she had anticipated and would unfortunately arrive at the cottage, now only five miles down the road, after dark. Maybe Darren had understated the case, maybe she should buy two cars, one for him and one for herself. But she was not going to think about Darren. Not now.

She pulled open the screen door of the restaurant and stepped inside, hearing it snap shut behind her and blinking a little in the bright light. A battery of heads, predominantly male, swung round to face her. Some turned away almost immediately, for Laura's looks, as Keith was apt to put it, were not the type to cause traffic jams. A few, more discerning, looked again at the slim, straight figure in the cotton pants and military-styled shirt, her dark hair tousled by the wind, her bearing unconsciously graceful.

Laura chose a table by the window, wondering if she would ever feel totally comfortable walking into a

23

restaurant alone. Eating was a companionable act, meant to be shared. Normally when she knew she would be eating alone she brought a book. But her books, including the texts that Jane had not wanted her to bring, were locked in the car and she did not feel like going out to get one. She picked up the menu instead.

The waitress had a long, sad face and the doleful eyes of a spaniel. She was breathing heavily, as if she had just run from the kitchen at top speed: far from the case. 'Evenin',' she wheezed. 'Wanna order?'

The cooking had better be good, thought Laura, who had had time to notice that neither the floor nor her water glass were as clean as they could be. 'Tomato juice, the roast turkey dinner, and apple pie with coffee, please.'

Her tongue between her teeth, clutching the pencil as if it were a lethal weapon, the waitress laboriously wrote all this down. Then she disappeared between swinging wooden doors at the back of the restaurant through which issued the clatter of pans and a loud, cheerful female voice talking, apparently, nonstop . . . Annie?

Having nothing else to do, Laura looked around. The truckdrivers were seated in a group at the far side of the room, shovelling food into their mouths with the air of men who mean business. Six teenagers, three boys and three girls, were sharing three milk shakes with a great deal of giggling and innuendo. Two overweight women, one unfortunately wearing tight pale pink slacks, were seated at the end of the counter. Each had a cup of coffee and a large piece of cream pie. They were talking in such low, solemn voices that Laura flippantly decided they must be discussing the shortcomings of their husbands.

There was one other person in the restaurant, whom, instinctively, she had left until the last. He, too, was sitting on a stool at the counter, beside the cash register and the rack of chocolate bars and chewing-gum. He looked comfortable and at ease, encased in his own private thoughts. Why, then, should she think he looked out of place in this shabby little restaurant, as out of place as, conversely, Darren would be at the Ritz. There was no concrete reason for her conclusion. His clothes, a frayed denim jacket and faded jeans, were as shabby as the restaurant. There was a stubble of beard on his chin. But his thick blond hair shone with cleanliness, and his profile, which was turned to her, was clean-cut, full of strength and character.

As if he felt her gaze upon him, he turned his head. His eyes were grey, the steel-grey of the sea at dusk. They passed over her indifferently, as though she were part of the furnishings, then resumed their contemplation of his clasped hands on the countertop.

Quickly Laura looked away. Her cheeks were flushed. She had been gawking at him like a starstruck teenager, she thought crossly, and in one impassive glance he had managed to make her feel rude, gauche, and much younger than twenty-five. A glance like that would do wonders at the Ritz.

Fortunately the waitress arrived, lugging the tray with tomato juice and a basket of rolls as if it bore a six-course meal. The tomato juice was chilled, tangy with Worcestershire sauce, and the rolls, piping hot, were deliciously light. Laura ate two and began to feel better. Once again the truckdrivers had been proved right.

The rest of the meal was equally good, for the turkey was tender and juicy, the vegetables fresh, and the gravy had never seen the inside of a tin. By the time she reached the apple pie, which had a crust flakier than any pastry she had ever made, the truckdrivers and the teenagers had left. An old man with a suspiciously red nose had come in and sprawled himself at a table near the counter. He had been served coffee and a muffin, and was interspersing loud slurps of coffee with bursts of song which the waitress was ignoring as if she had heard him many times before. The women were on their third cup of coffee, while the man by the cash register, like her, had just been served dessert. Laura did not want to leave at the same time as him. She ate the pie more quickly than it deserved, gulped her coffee and looked at the bill. For the amount and the quality of the food the price was very reasonable, so reasonable that it was hard to imagine how Annie was making much of a profit. Picking up her shoulder bag, Laura pushed back her chair and walked over to the cash register.

The man in the denim jacket was adding sugar to his coffee. Two packages of sugar, one after the other. Fascinated, Laura watched him tear open a third. Such over-indulgence, while it did not seem to go with the austere profile, did make him more human. Hurriedly she looked away before he could catch her staring again. But in her mind's eye remained an image of impressively broad shoulders under the undistinguished jacket and of crisp blond hair curling at his nape. Flustered by her own thoughts, she looked around for the waitress.

The old man called out blearily, 'Join me, dearie. Annie's muffins are——' he paused for a belch, '—a feast for the gods. Nectar! Ambrosia! From the land of milk and honey.' Another belch.

Said Laura, smiling at him politely over her shoulder, 'No, thank you. I have to get on my way.'

A large-bosomed woman with a mass of orange curls had emerged from the kitchen. 'Now, Archie, you stop that,' she scolded. 'I've told you before you're not to go bothering the customers. And you've been at the bottle again, after all your fine promises. What am I to do with you?' Without pausing for breath she switched her attention to Laura. 'And was everything satisfactory?'

Laura gave her a warm smile. 'Wonderful! The apple pie was out of this world.' She passed over the bill and unzipped her handbag, reaching in for her wallet.

He handbag, as usual, was crammed with everything from make-up to rolls of film. She fumbled for the bulk of her wallet, frowning a little. Notepad. Chequebook. Pencils and pens. Hairbrush. But no wallet.

Her frown deepened. She pulled the zipper fully open and gave the bag a good shake. The extra set of keys rattled. She saw a tube of lipstick she thought she had lost and a bill she hadn't paid. She did not see her wallet.

Panic-stricken she scrabbled among the contents of the bag. A pencil dropped to the floor and rolled under the counter. She grabbed at an untidy bunch of tissues before they could do the same, and said faintly, 'I think I've lost my wallet.'

Silence greeted her statement. She looked up to find Annie staring at her, hands on her hips, eyes wary. Laura blushed, reading Annie's thoughts as clearly as if the woman had spoken them. Annie thought this was a trick. Annie thought she was trying to get away without paying for her meal.

Passing behind the blond-haired man, Laura plunked herself down two seats away from him and tipped out her bag on the counter. Among the indiscriminate jumble of contents her wallet was conspicuously absent. She had known by now that she wouldn't find it but had felt she had to try. Rounding up all her paraphernalia, she shoved it back in her handbag and said helplessly, 'Truly—I've lost my wallet . . . I took it out at the gas station when I paid for the fan belt. I must have left it there. I could write you a cheque.'

Annie, who had moved to stand in front of her, waved a well-muscled arm at a sign on the wall, which in untidy print declared, 'No Credit. No Cheques. Thank you. The Management.'

Briefly Laura closed her eyes. She could say, 'I won the lottery two weeks ago, a million dollars. My cheque won't bounce.' But she did not. She was quite sure Annie would not believe her. Annie wanted cash now, not talk of a million dollars. She opened her eyes and said with all the sincerity she could muster, 'I'm not trying to cheat you, please believe me. I really have lost my wallet. I don't know the name of the gas station but——' And then she remembered the folding wooden sign by the gas pumps. 'Hours 8 a.m. to 8 p.m. Closed on Sundays.' Looking at her watch, she saw that it was nearly nine-thirty.

'The gas station's closed by now,' she went on desperately. 'But I'm staying——'

From behind her Archie, full of whiskey and bonhomie, offered loudly, 'Put it on my bill, Annie. The pension comes in day after tomorrow. 'S been a long time since I bought a meal for a pretty girl.'

'You stay out of this, Archie. Your pension's no better than your promises, here today and gone tomorrow.'

Laura began again. 'I'm staying at a cottage down the road. I can give you the name of the owners and the 'phone number—I'll be there a month. Once I've gone back to the gas station tomorrow I can pay for my meal.'

For the first time the man in the denim jacket raised his head. He looked Laura up and down, his grey eyes full of contempt. 'How convenient that the gas station's closed,' he said.

Laura had time to think, Just my luck to meet the most attractive man I've ever seen, under circumstances like this, before saying with dangerous politeness, 'Why don't you mind your own business?'

'Annie's a friend of mine. I don't like to see her cheated.'

'I am *not* trying to cheat her!'

'Come off it—it's the oldest trick in the book.' Another of those scathing up-and-down surveys. 'Is that how you afford leather sandals and nice clothes? By cheating people who work hard to make an honest living? And do you think Archie is going to pay for what he's getting? Of course he's not. He's here because Annie won't turn him away, because she's a decent woman who cares about people and who deserves better than someone like you!'

Annie shifted uncomfortably. 'Now, Chuck, you don't——'

But Laura had had enough. Overriding Annie's stentorian contralto—no mean feat—she snarled, 'I don't know who you are, Chuck, or who appointed you judge and jury, but——'

'The name is Charles.'

'She called you Chuck. And stop interrupting!'

'I hate being called Chuck.'

Annie interposed with magisterial calm, 'You don't look like a Charles. Chuck suits you better. So that's what I'll call you.'

'You're quite wrong,' Laura spat. 'He's a Charles to the bone. And what the *hell* are we doing discussing his name, anyway? We're supposed to be talking about my wallet!'

Unexpectedly Annie began to laugh, a booming laugh as rich as her voice. 'Anyone who can take you on, Chuck, deserves a break.' As her laugh lifted the mounds of her cheeks, her eyes twinkled and her bright curls bounced. Laura gaped at her, and heard herself addressed. 'Where'd you say you were staying?'

'At Sally and Bill Cunningham's cottage. Five miles down the road.' Once again she fumbled in her purse. 'I've got the 'phone number written down in my book.'

The breath escaped between Charles's teeth in a long hiss. 'That's all I bloody well need,' he said.

Laura glowered at him. 'I've got a perfect right to stay there. Sally's sister is my best friend. Not that it's any concern of yours.'

He gave her a thoroughly nasty smile. 'I'm afraid you're mistaken. Allow me to introduce myself. Your next-door neighbour, Charles—not Chuck—Richards at your service.'

The brown eyes with their fringe of dark lashes widened in dismay. 'Oh, no!' Laura gasped. 'Are you living in the other cottage? The only other cottage on the peninsula?'

'I am.' His eyes gleamed derisively. 'We share the driveway and the beach.'

'I came here to get away from everyone,' she wailed.

'Solitude. Peace and quiet. And now I've got *you* for a neighbour.'

Charles glanced up at Annie, who had been listening with unabashed interest. 'She's not very flattering, is she, Annie, my love?'

'Chuck, sometimes you've got a look that can blister paint,' said Annie. 'Can't say I blame her.'

'Dear me,' Laura said limpidly. 'Deserted on all sides, Chuck. Or does Archie think you're wonderful?'

Not the slightest bit put out, Charles reached in the back pocket of his jeans and pulled out a leather wallet. 'I'm sure he does. Annie, make up my bill, love. I'll pay hers as well. As her next-door neighbour, I'm sure I can collect. One way or another.' The grey eyes slid over Laura's flushed cheeks and parted lips. 'By the way, shouldn't you introduce yourself? It's not very polite of me to refer to you as *her*.'

'I quite agree, it's not,' Laura responded with a saccharine smile. 'Although on the basis of our admittedly brief acquaintance, it's more or less what I'd expect.' She saw laughter spark his eyes, tried very hard to think about Bart, and added, 'My name is Laura. Laura Walker.'

He stood up and held out his hand. 'Delighted to meet you. I can see that the beach is going to be a much more interesting place.'

Laura, perforce, stood up, too. He was as tall as Darren; it wasn't fair, she thought, as her hand was swallowed in his. Regrettably she liked the warmth and firmness of his palm against hers. She also liked the strength of his grip, and discovered that there was just as much character in his face head-on as there had been in profile. Then Archie belched again and the spell was broken. She pulled back her hand and said stiffly, 'Now that Annie knows I'm not going to vanish into the night, there's no need for you to pay for my meal. I'll go back to the gas station in the morning and pay her then. Annie, that will be all right with you, won't it?'

'Sure, dear,' said Annie, watching the stubborn line

of Charles's mouth. 'It's all right with *me.*'

Charles put a couple of notes on the counter. 'That's to pay for both of us. Put Archie's on it too.'

Annie rolled her eyes, rang in the totals on the old-fashioned register and gave Charles the change. 'There you go,' she said, sneaking a quick glance at Laura's furious face. 'Your good deed for the day, Chuck.' She lifted her voice, unnecessarily, considering the dimensions of the room. 'Nearly closing time, Archie.'

'I'll give you a drive home, Archie,' Charles said, and raised a sardonic eyebrow at Laura. 'It was my pleasure, Miss Walker.'

'If you think I'm going to thank you for something I didn't want you to do, you're wrong.'

'Pay as you go—it's always been my motto.'

'Under normal circumstances it's mine as well,' Laura grated. 'As you insist on making such a grand gesture, kindly leave a tip for the waitress on my table. Good night, Mr Richards. Good night, Archie. Annie, I'll see you tomorrow, and I promise I'll have my wallet.' Swinging her bag over her shoulder, her cheeks red with temper, she stalked out of the restaurant. As the screen door squealed shut behind her, a cloud of moths rose from the light over the door.

A black and grey Jeep was parked on the other side of the building. No doubt Mr Charles Richards's Jeep. Although it was splattered with mud, it was not an old or a cheap vehicle, and almost against her will Laura found herself wondering about Charles Richards. His voice was that of an educated man, his hands were well-kept, and he had an unconscious air of self-confidence that was as much a part of him, she was sure, as the straight nose and the firm jaw. Yet his clothes were patched and worn, and he was on friendly terms with a man who was presumably the local drunk. As if to punctuate her thoughts the screen door opened to another fluttering of moths and Archie stepped outside, somewhat unsteadily. He was singing again, and as she caught a couple of stray words she blushed and hastened to unlock the car door.

Across the parking lot Charles Richards called out, 'If you want to wait here, Laura, it'll only take me a few minutes to take Archie home. Then you could follow me to the cottages, you might have difficulty finding them in the dark.'

No doubt it was a well-meant offer, and had she been sweet-natured like Sue-Ann she would have thanked him and accepted. But Laura was still seething from his assumption that she had tried to cheat Annie, and was not about to forgive him. 'No, thank you,' she said clearly. 'Jane gave me very good directions. I'm sure I can find my way.'

He gave her a mocking salute, grabbed Archie and levered him into the passenger seat, and a moment later drove away in the direction from which Laura had come. When the tail-lights had disappeared, Laura got in her Honda and started off in the opposite direction.

Annie's restaurant had been one of the landmarks in Jane's careful set of directions, for the driveway to the cottages was on the left-hand side of the road five and a half miles from the restaurant. Jane did not look kindly upon the government's change to the metric system and consequently persisted in measuring distances in miles, whereas Laura's car gave distances only in kilometres. Trying to figure out in her head how many kilometres equalled 5.5 miles, Laura drove slowly along the winding road. Occasionally a light shone through the darkness and she would see a small frame house or a mobile home set back from the road in the woods. But for the most part she saw only trees topped by a star-spangled sky, trees that in the daylight would reveal themselves as spruce, birch and fir, but that at night blended into an amorphous black mass, solid and threatening, into which Laura would not have ventured for—for a million dollars, she thought with a weak smile.

Jane's only other landmark was a big oak tree, beyond which a gravelled driveway turned down towards the sea. Laura was city-bred, and although four years in Grantham had taught her what elm trees looked like and how to tell an apple orchard from a pear orchard, she was not well-acquainted with oaks, particularly in the pitch dark; and botany had always been the necessary but boring part of biology that one had to sit through in order to get to zoology. She had gone a little over eight kilometres when she saw on the left side of the road a huge hardwood whose spreading limbs canopied a narrow dirt track which vanished into the darkness in the direction of the sea. She slowed the car, flicking on the turn-signal and peering down the track. The cottages were not visible from the road, so Jane had said. It was one of their charms. This must be the turn-off.

She left the road and drove slowly down the track, clutching the steering wheel. The track was narrower than it had looked, so narrow that branches scraped against the sides of her car. She lurched through a series of potholes, wincing as the underside of the Honda rasped against rock. The road should divide soon, one branch going to Jane's sister's cottage, one to Charles Richards's. But the road did not divide. If anything it got narrower. Then she saw ahead of her, low to the ground, the gleam of yellow eyes.

She slammed on the brakes. A cat with matted grey fur slunk off the road and dived into the underbrush.

A cat means civilisation, thought Laura, trying to ignore the racing of her heart and not succeeding. What's the matter, Laura? Are you scared of the dark?

Quickly, before she could answer her own question in the affirmative, she let out the clutch and drove on. Ferns as tall as children brushed the windows of the car with delicate green fingers; the stars had disappeared, blanked out by the arching boughs of spruce overhead. And then Laura's suspicion that she was on the wrong road was abruptly confirmed when she saw ahead of her, lying across the track, a gigantic spruce tree, the base of its trunk splintered and torn by the force of a long-ago storm.

No cottages down here, Laura thought in disgust. You'd better find out what an oak tree looks like. Putting the gear lever into reverse, she very slowly began to back out the way she had come. She was almost to the main road when she saw another vehicle parked on the shoulder, waiting for her. A black and grey Jeep with a man in a denim jacket standing by the hood.

She muttered a rude word under her breath, swung back on to the paved road and pulled up behind him. In a leisurely fashion he walked round to her window. She rolled it down and said crisply, 'Yes, I took the wrong road, and thank you, I will follow you.'

He glanced over his shoulder and drawled, 'You're supposed to turn in by an oak tree. That's maple.'

'How was I supposed to know the difference?'

'The red leaf on the Canadian flag?' he hazarded.

'I dislike nationalistic symbols.' She glanced at him through her lashes. 'I think they do more to divide than to unite.'

'I think you're a young woman with a great many decided opinions.'

'One of which is that I'm tired and would very much like to get to the cottage.'

'We shall lie on the beach with tall glasses of rum and orange and discuss nationalism, you and I.'

'I drink gin.' She gave him a cool smile. 'And I prefer to be asked for dates. Not told.'

'Ah yes . . . it was solitude you were craving. You might find, Laura Walker, that you'll be glad of my company after a few days of isolation at the cottage.'

'The place is that bad, is it?'

He began to laugh. He looked very handsome when he laughed. His teeth were beautiful, white and even, as well cared for as his hair and his hands. 'Do you always give as good as you get?' he asked.

'When you've spent four years bringing up three teenagers, you learn the fine art of self-preservation.' It was the first remark of a personal nature Laura had made to him and almost immediately she regretted it, for she saw the sharpening of interest in his eyes.

But all he said was, 'We can discuss that as well as nationalism. It might even be more interesting. Now, why don't you follow me? I'll go right to your cottage so I can help you open it up and carry your stuff in—and don't argue, Laura Walker. Despite my appearance I can behave like a perfect gentleman.'

She said with the utmost truth, 'I'm sure you can.'

The smile faded from his face. 'What do you mean?' he said sharply.

She frowned a little. 'I don't know ... for some reason I think you'd be just as much at home at the Ritz as you were at Annie's restuarant. Don't ask me why.'

He, too, was frowning, two short vertical lines marking his forehead, and for a moment she was sure he was going to fling another question at her. Then his lips compressed. 'The turn-off's only a few hundred yards up the road, so I'll go slowly.'

Wondering at his reaction, she watched him stride back to the Jeep and swing himself up into it, his jeans pulled taut around his legs. He had very long legs. She felt, and was horrified at herself, a stirring of desire. Only last week she had been weeping over Bart. How could she now be lusting after a blond-haired stranger who had virtually accused her of being a liar and who was as full of contradictions as an oak tree had acorns? Good simile, Laura. Tomorrow morning she would take a long, careful look at the oak tree. Botany might turn out to be a necessity up here.

The oak tree was massive, its trunk wide of girth, black and ridged. The road to the cottages was very different from the track she had followed earlier; it was wider and smoothly gravelled, just as Jane had said. When it divided into two, the Jeep took the left fork. In the swing of the headlights Laura caught her first glimpse of the cottage, which had white shingles and dark green shutters and a huge beachstone chimney at one corner; trellises supported the drooping branches of the old-fashioned rosebushes. It looked so friendly and approachable that Laura's fingers relaxed their hold on the steering wheel and she gave a tiny sigh of relief. Her holiday had begun disastrously, but everything was going to be all right.

She pulled up beside the Jeep and got out. The gentlest of breezes was whispering among the treetops, while from the shore came another, more rhythmic whisper, that of waves caressing the beach. The air smelled of the sea; once again she could see the stars.

'It's so quiet,' Laura said finally in a hushed, soft voice.

Charles had been watching her. 'Did you really lose your wallet?' he said curtly.

The peaceful spell of the summer night was broken. Yet it was not anger Laura felt this time as much as hurt. She answered his question with one of her own. 'Are you always such a sceptic?'

'I've seen plenty to be sceptical about.'

'Single-handedly I cannot possibly restore your faith in human nature.'

'Try me.'

'You're a very strange man,' she said slowly. 'I don't understand you.'

'You're changing the subject, Laura. Come on—try me.'

She raised her eyes to his and said in the tone of voice she had often used with Darren, 'I told Annie the absolute truth. Somewhere between the gas station where I got a new fan belt and her restuarant I lost my wallet. It is my sincere hope that I left it at the gas station and that the proprietor was honest enough to keep it for me.' She shrugged. 'That's it. I can well afford to pay for my own meals and I don't go around cheating people.' Despite her best intentions some of the hurt showed in her voice.

'Then I owe you an apology.'

'Hadn't you better wait until tomorrow? I might drive away in the night and never be heard of again.'

'I don't think you will . . . I'm sorry for what I said in the restaurant, Laura. I jumped to all the wrong conclusions.'

It was a generous apology, straight forward and to the point, for which she could only respect him. 'You're forgiven,' she said lightly, although her brown eyes remained very serious.

'Thank you.' He drew a deep breath. 'Are you tired?'

Once again the gentle whisper of the waves reached Laura's ears. 'I was, yes. But not anymore.' She glanced up at the tangled glitter of the stars. 'I think this is going to be a wonderful place.'

'Why don't I show you the path to the beach?'

'Now?'

'Sure—why not?'

She gave a delighted laugh. 'Why not, indeed?'

'Here, take my hand.'

She hesitated fractionally. It was one thing to shake hands with him in a well-lit restaurant under Annie's watchful eyes, quite another to hold hands in the murmurous darkness of a summer night.

She should have know he would notice. She held out her hand and felt again the clasp of his lean fingers. He led her past the Jeep and down a pathway between the trees where the ground was springy with fallen needles, and as they went the whisper of the waves became the full-fledged voice of the sea: the thud and splash as the water curled and fell, the hiss and seethe of foam on the sand. The path opened into a grassy field, separated from the beach by a ridge of shale. Laura slid down the far side of the ridge and felt the softness of sand beneath her feet. She let go of Charles's hand and bent to remove her sandals, wriggling her toes with childish pleasure as she rolled up the hem of her trousers. Without saying a word she began to walk down the sand towards the sea, unable to resist the lure of its age-old patterns of tides and currents that are never different yet never the same. For a moment she was silent, awed by the inky obscurity of the sky and the

the shining blackness of the sea, polished like ebony. Then a wave encircled her feet and she gave an undignified shriek. 'It's freezing!'

Behind her Charles said, 'It'll warm up by September.'

'That won't do me any good, I'm only here for a month.'

'You get used to it after a while.' He grinned at her. 'Once you turn numb.'

'You don't mean to say you swim in that?'

'Every morning. Wakes me up.'

'Haven't you heard of hypothermia?'

He flexed his arms. 'I'm tough, Laura.'

She gave a sudden, breathless laugh. 'You know, if someone had told me this morning before I left that by nightfall I'd be standing on the beach with a very large and very handsome male who was busy showing off his muscles, I'd have told them they were crazy.'

She saw instantly that she had disconcerted him. His arms fell to his sides. 'Well . . . that's a nice compliment. The handsome part, I mean.'

She felt even more breathless and unconsciously stepped back a pace. As a girl Sue-Ann's age she had always had a tendency to speak before she thought. Four years in Grantham had taught her a measure of discretion, or so she had believed. What was it about Charles Richards that made her neglect the lessons of those four years and say whatever came into her head? 'It must be late,' she said nervously. 'I'd better get my stuff out of the car.'

'It's okay, Laura, I'm not going to jump on you. And I'll help you carry your things in.'

'I can manage.' For she had remembered something: her two suitcases had address labels on them. She did not want Charles Richards knowing she was from Grantham, where the winner of the latest million-dollar lottery lived. Although her name was ordinary enough, her name coupled with a place might trigger his memory. She wanted to be accepted by Charles as an ordinary young woman, not as a very rich young woman; it was already quite astonishingly important to her that this should be so.

'You're very independent,' he said, moving a little closer to her.

He was looming over her, a dark shadow against all the other shadows of the night. Laura swallowed, wondering if his lips would be as warm and firm as his hands. Somehow she did not think she was going to find out. At the same time she wondered at her own behaviour. She had not looked at another man besides Bart for years ... what was wrong with her? She said as casually as she could, 'Is independence to be applauded or deplored?'

'Applauded, by all means. Up to a point. There comes a time when we all need people ... Why are you so nervous?'

She jumped. 'I'm not!'

He took another step closer. 'I think you are.'

Her feet seemed to have grown roots into the sand. 'Why should I be nervous? You've assured me you're a gentleman,' she said with as much composure as she could muster. 'You'd better be—or I'll tell Annie on you.'

'The ultimate threat!' The smile left his face. 'I don't feel very gentlemanly, Laura. I feel like kissing you, if you want the truth. But I suppose the fact that I'm talking about it rather than doing it means I'm not ready to take the risk. Because I'm sure you're perfectly capable of slapping my face.'

Or kissing you back ... 'A wise decision,' she remarked, hoping she sounded suitably light-hearted.

'Oh, wisdom ... wisdom doesn't have much to do with a man and a woman on the beach on a summer's night.' Irritably he shrugged his shoulders under the denim jacket. 'Let's go back.'

This time Charles did not take her hand, but climbed up the shale and strode across the field without even looking to see if Laura was following. She was. But her mind was in a turmoil, her body suddenly aching with tiredness. Too much had happened in one day. To be bewitched by a handsome stranger had not been among her plans for the month in Cape Breton . . .

When they reached the cottage, Charles got a torch out of the Jeep and stood patiently while she found her keys, unlocked the door, and turned on the lights. 'A friend of Annie's was over last week and gave the place a good cleaning,' he said. 'So everything's in working order.'

'It looks great,' she said from the doorway, giving the living room the once-over.

'Good night then, Laura.'

'Good night,' she replied. But she said it to his back because he was already getting into the Jeep. For the second time that evening she watched him drive away. The trees soon muffled the sound of the motor and masked the twin beams of the lights. The other cottage was not as near as she had thought.

Resolutely Laura got her luggage out of the car, making several trips to carry everything inside. Then she locked the door, gave the whole cottage a cursory examination, dragged her nightdress out of one of the suitcases and fell into bed. Her last waking thought was not of Bart, nor of her nephews and niece in Grantham, nor of Annie of the hennaed eyebrows. It was of Charles Richards, who had been so disarmingly pleased when she had told him he was handsome.

CHAPTER THREE

LAURA did not sleep particularly well. The bed was harder than she was used to, and the wind came up in the night, causing the cottage to creak and groan alarmingly. The old house in Grantham had its own collection of noises, but Laura was accustomed to those. These were new noises, and lying alone in the middle of the night it was all too easy to transpose the rapping of a tree branch against the side of the house into the sound of human knuckles, or the squeak of floorboards into slow, stealthy footsteps. At dawn she fell asleep. But she was awake two hours later because that was when she always woke up in order to get Sue-Ann up for school and the boys off to work.

You're on holiday, she adjured herself, and closed her eyes, burying her head under the covers because the sun was shining. But it did no good. A whole flock of birds was practising early morning trills outside her window, sounding like an orchestra tuning up. The waves murmured on the shore. And unfortunately her wallet was still lost.

It was probably the wallet more than the birds or the waves that got Laura out of bed, for she was well aware that she would not truly begin to feel she was on holiday until she had found it. Pulling on a housecoat she padded to the tiny bathroom, where she was pleased to discover that the shower produced a plentiful supply of hot water.

The cottage had two bedrooms, both with double beds, pine blanket boxes, and braided rugs on the uneven board floors. A stone fireplace filled one corner of the living room, while a table and chairs had been placed by the picture windows which overlooked the meadow and the ocean. The chintz-covered chesterfield and armchairs co-existed amiably with the faded, striped rug, like old friends who have been together for many years.

The kitchen equipment was basic but adequate. Unfortunately all the cupboards were empty, as was the tiny refrigerator. Trying to ignore the growling of her stomach and the fact that she would not have any money to buy groceries or breakfast until she had retrieved her wallet, Laura went in search of the telephone.

The telephone book was on a coffee table by the chesterfield, the kind of coffee table made by schoolboys in industrial arts; the telephone was attached to the wall near the kitchen. Because she remembered the brand of gasoline and the name of the village, Laura had no trouble finding the number for the service station. She picked up the receiver to dial the operator since it was a long-distance call.

But the telephone was dead. No click, no dial tone, nothing. *Disconnected*, thought Laura in frustration. Which made sense. Why would Jane's sister pay for a telephone she wasn't here to use?

Now what was she going to do? She didn't want to drive a hundred miles to the gas station only to find her wallet had not been found. She had to 'phone first. She went into the bedroom and searched her handbag and her pockets, coming up with two pennies, a nickel and several theatre stubs. Seven cents was not enough to use a pay 'phone, she had to have a dime.

She had two choices. She could go to the other cottage and ask to use Charles's 'phone—if he had one. Or she could to go the restaurant and ask Annie to lend her a dime. Of the two courses of action the latter seemed the more distasteful. Charles it would have to be.

Fifteen minutes later, dressed in a flowered cotton skirt and a white T-shirt, Laura was climbing the steps of the other cottage. Its shutters were red rather than

green and it lacked the rosebushes, but it was otherwise
the twin to hers.

Music was pouring through the screen door, music
that she recognised, having been well educated by
Keith. Wagner at eight o'clock in the morning, she
thought. Oh, no ... Banging her fist on the door
frame to override Sieglinde's full-voiced lament, and
irresistibly reminded of Annie, who definitely had
Wagnerian elements to her character, she waited for a
response. One thing was sure. Charles couldn't be
asleep.

The response was not long in coming. A man's naked
body interposed itself between the mesh of the screen
door and the living room beyond. Laura blinked,
grabbed the railing for support and said weakly, 'Good
morning, Charles.'

He pushed the door open. 'Hi, Laura. Come in.'

He was not completely naked. A pair of very brief
blue swim trunks just covered the strategic areas. But
the general effect was overwhelming. As Laura sidled
through the door, Wotan, King of the gods, began to
reproach Brünnhilde for her disobedience. Laura took a
deep breath, smelled the delicious aromas of fresh
coffee and frying bacon and blurted, not looking at
Charles, 'May I use your 'phone?'

'What's wrong?' he said in a puzzled tone of voice.

'I have to 'phone the service station to see if my
wallet's there. The 'phone at my place is disconnected
and I've only got seven cents to my name.'

'That wasn't what I meant. Look at me, Laura.'

'Do I have to?' she gasped.

He took her by the arm. 'Laura . . .?'

Glancing up at him, she said fretfully, 'I just wasn't
expecting to see quite so much of you this early in the
morning.' Her eyes dropped from his, found themselves
at the level of his hair-covered chest and skidded
sideways.

'You're acting as if you've never seen a man in
swimming trunks before.'

'Of course I have!' She repeated lamely, 'I wasn't expecting it, that's all.'

He slid his other hand around her elbow. 'You're very good for my ego.'

'I'm sure your ego gets lots of attention.' Not to mention the rest of you.

'As they say in *Porgy and Bess*, it ain't necessarily so . . .'

'What you're playing now isn't *Porgy and Bess*.'

He laughed. 'Don't you like Wagner?'

'Occasionally. In small doses. Gershwin is more to my taste.'

His hands tightened a little. 'We're avoiding the issue. To get back to my ego—you don't even know who I am, Laura. I could be a beach bum. Riffraff. A layabout. A ne'er-do-well.'

She stared fixedly at the tangled blond hair springing from his smoothly tanned skin. 'I don't think you're any of those things.'

'I could be unemployed. On the dole.'

It was her turn to look puzzled. 'I don't understand what you're getting to.'

'You've been kind enough to imply you don't find me unattractive. Don't you want to know something about my financial status first?'

She pulled free, thoroughly bewildered. 'First? What do you mean, first? I'm not planning to marry you or— or anything else. Sure, I find you attractive. That's not a crime, is it? And it's certainly nothing to do with your financial status.'

'You mean if you met two men whom you found equally attractive and one had lots of money and the other had very little, you wouldn't go for the one with the money?'

'That's a totally artificial situation and you know it!' She thought of her own financial status and added, 'I might very well choose the other one. Money changes people. Not always for the best. Now please will you let me use your 'phone or do I have to ask you to lend me a dime so I can use Annie's?'

'Annie doesn't open the restaurant until noon . . . hell, the bacon's burning!' He loped away from her towards the stove, grabbing the handle of the pan and pulling it off the element, yelping as some hot fat spattered on his bare flesh. With a fork he held up a blackened strip of bacon. 'Damn it—who would want to eat that?'

Her mouth was watering. 'I might. If offered.'

He frowned. 'Haven't you had breakfast?'

'I didn't bring any groceries and I don't have any money to buy them.'

He stared at her in consternation. 'I'm sorry, Laura, I never thought of that last night or I'd have invited you over here for breakfast this morning. I'll put some more bacon on. Help yourself to coffee, the mugs are in the corner cupboard.'

She wanted to stay. Very much. But she had the horrible feeling that if she had to squeeze between him and the counter to get to the coffee and the mugs, she would find her hands reaching out to stroke the flat planes of his back and the long hollow of his spine. I must be mad, she thought frantically, and said with as much composure as she could manage, 'Do you mind if I 'phone the garage first? If I know they've got my wallet, my mind will be more at ease.'

'The 'phone's in my bedroom. Have you got the number?'

'Yes, thanks.' She began to back away. 'I won't be long.'

He put down the packet of bacon. 'Wait a minute,' he said, his grey eyes quizzical. 'Would you feel more comfortable if I put on some clothes?'

Laura felt the blush begin somewhere in the vicinity of her throat and scorch its way up her cheeks. 'I—yes, I would.'

He came a little closer. 'You're no city-sophisticate, are you? Laura, are you married or engaged or living common-law or otherwise spoken for?'

Another unexpected question. 'Not really. Someone

asked me to marry him just before I came up here. That's one of the reasons I came—I needed time to think about it.'

'If you need to think about it, don't do it. Simple.'

'Sure,' she said ironically. 'Just like that.'

Charles came another step closer, and Laura fought the urge to retreat, unaware that the battle was reflected in her eyes. He said, 'Does he tell you how beautiful you are?'

Only since I won the lottery ... She quoted Keith with perfect accuracy, 'One of my nephews says I'll never cause a traffic jam.'

'Does he? Interesting ... because when I saw you at a distance in the restaurant, I would have agreed with him. But standing close to you like this I can see the way your eyes tilt at the corners and the little gold flecks in the irises. Your mouth is exquisitely shaped ... and, of course, you blush beautifully.' His face was straight but devilment sparked his eyes. 'Should I take the risk now, that I wanted to take last night?'

She knew exactly what he meant. In an unsettling mixture of panic and excitement she said, 'I can't possibly make that decision for you.'

He had dropped his hands on her shoulders, his face only inches from hers. 'Will you accept my decision either way?'

Her lashes drifted to her cheeks. Recklessly she decided to tell the truth. 'I do have a preference.'

'Do you, now? I believe I know what it is.'

'Try me ...' she whispered.

His lips were warm and firm, their pressure tentative then deepening. His hands stayed at her shoulders so that their bodies were three or four inches apart. Yet when he released her after what could have been moments or minutes, Laura was aware of an inner trembling and a sense that standing motionless in the sunlit kitchen she had travelled a very long way.

The devilment had vanished from Charles's eyes; they

were intensely serious. 'Well,' he said inadequately. 'Well . . .'

Laura could not think of anything to say, even anything as uninspiring and unoriginal as 'Well.' She tried to smile, found that her lips were feflecting her inner trembling and lowered her eyes to the blond hair on his chest.

He said after what seemed a prolonged silence, 'That wasn't quite what I'd expected.'

He had given her her cue. 'What had you expected?'

He shifted restlessly. 'Oh, I don't know . . . a casual kiss, I suppose. I certainly hàdn't anticipated the earth would move.'

The orchestra was thundering in the background. 'Maybe it was the music,' she suggested.

'What happened to me a moment ago was nothing to do with Wagner.' He tilted her chin with one finger. 'Did it happen to you, Laura?'

'Couldn't you tell?'

'Did it, Laura?'

'Yes,' she whispered. 'Yes, it did.'

'And is it like that when you're kissed by the man back home who wants to marry you?'

'No.' Her eyes widened in appalled recognition. 'No, it isn't like that at all.'

'Another reason not to marry him,' Charles said flatly. His hand fell to his side. 'I'll go and put some clothes on, then you can make your 'phone call.'

She watched him walk away from her. He was broad-shouldered, narrow-hipped, and long of leg—altogether beautiful. She closed her eyes, feeling the music swirl around her and envelop her in its passionate fury, wondering if anything would ever be the same again . . .

'What are you thinking about?'

Her eyes jerked open. Charles was now wearing faded jeans and a cotton shirt whose cuffs he was rolling up. 'Nothing in particular,' she stammered. 'You're bad for my thought processes.'

'I know the feeling ... Laura, there's something I
want to ask you. What did you mean when you said
money changes people?'

Not for anything was she going to tell him about
her million-dollar win. If she was to be the recipient
of another of those dazzling kisses she had to know
she was being kissed for herself, not for her money.
'Oh, I don't know. It's just a feeling I have—that to
have more money than you need is not necessarily a
good thing.'

'The problem is to decide how much you need.'

She didn't want to discuss money. 'You're right, of
course,' she said dismissively. 'And to get down to
basics, I need my wallet. Because I like eating. Will you
excuse me?'

She walked across the living room. His view was the
twin of hers, and the furniture had the same
comfortable shabbiness. But the room was a great deal
untidier than hers. Books, magazines, clothes, used
dishes, sand-caked running shoes, crumpled towels ...
Charles Richards was not a tidy man. His bedroom
bore out her conclusion. The clothes he had been
wearing last night were in a heap on the floor. The bed
was unmade, a tangle of sheets; when she saw the single
hollow in the pillow, she felt her knees grow weak.

The telephone was on an upended orange crate that
served as a bedside table. She took out the little fold of
paper on which she had written the number of the gas
station and dialled the operator to bill the call to her
home number. After a series of clicks she was
connected. 'Bentley's Esso,' said a man's voice.

Laura explained why she was calling. 'Hold on,' said
the man. 'I'll get Joe, he's the manager.'

Joe came on the line and again Laura explained her
predicament. 'Can you describe the wallet, ma'am?' Joe
asked.

As accurately as she could, Laura complied. Joe said
calmly, 'Okay. Yeah, we got it. You left it on the
counter. You gonna come and get it?'

'Thank goodness you've got it—I was afraid you wouldn't. Yes, I'll drive up this morning.'

'Okay, then. See you later.'

'Thank you, Joe.' She replaced the receiver, took one last glance at the tumbled bed and left the room.

Charles was frying more bacon in the kitchen. She smiled at him. 'They've got it! I left it on the counter, which wasn't very clever of me—thank goodness for honest people.'

'Of which you're one.' He was carefully flipping over two rashers of bacon.

'I have a feeling you are, as well,' she replied, speaking lightly yet knowing her words for the truth.

He looked over at her. 'I'm really sorry for what I said in the restaurant.'

'You're forgiven.' And because he had kissed her and her wallet was found and the bacon smelled delicious, she gave him a briliant smile.

He put down the fork he was holding, took a step towards her, halted in frustration and said, 'I'd like to kiss you again . . . hell, who am I kidding? I'd like to pick you up and carry you into the bedroom and make love to you. And, no, I am not in the habit of taking women I met less than twenty-four hours ago into my bed. Especially at eight-thirty in the morning.'

His directness evoked a similar directness in her. 'What's so special about me?' she said, which prevented her from saying, I'd like to make love to you, too.

'Damned if I know. Because you have a temper and you're not afraid to stick up for yourself? Because your beauty is quiet and unforced—like a wild flower rather than—than a hothouse orchid. Because you're——'

Suddenly she was laughing. 'Charles, you're going to burn the second lot of bacon!'

He swore under his breath, forked the bacon to one side of the pan and lowered the heat. 'I'm normally a fairly competent cook, believe it or not. One or two eggs?'

'One please. Turned over.'

'There's bread on the counter. Want to make some toast?'

She managed to get through the narrow space between him and the counter without actually touching him. *Without raping him, Laura. If he's behaving abnormally, so are you.* She found butter, jam and marmalade in the refrigerator along with an assortment of leftovers, some in an advanced state of deterioration. Closing the door, she remarked, 'Some of the things in there are alive.'

It was his turn to laugh. 'I know. I hate throwing anything out, but when suppertime comes it's so much easier to go up to Annie's. One of these days I'll give the whole kitchen a good cleaning. If you want to pour the coffee, we're ready to eat.'

She carried the coffee mugs into the living room, where Charles was moving the muddle of papers and books from the table to the floor. He produced two woven placemats and paper serviettes, and they sat down to eat.

Wagner, mercifully, was silent, Brünnhilde having been encircled by the ring of fire at the end of Act III. Charles passed Laura the salt and pepper and said, 'Tell me about this man who wants to marry you.'

Laura's fork remained poised halfway to her mouth. 'No!'

'Why not?'

'Because it's none of your business.'

'Yes, it is. I want to know about the opposition.'

'Charles, I came up here to get away from it all. To be by myself and think things out. Not to——'

'——be kissed at eight-thirty in the morning? You weren't exactly fighting me off, Laura.'

She reached for the marmalade, slathered her toast with it and capitulated. Better to discuss Bart than that kiss. 'His name is Bart Manning, he's twenty-eight years old and the town lawyer.'

'What does he look like?'

It was strangely difficult to recall exact details of Bart

with Charles Richards sitting across from her. She did her best. 'He's five-feet-eleven, dark brown hair and moustache, light blue eyes, good-looking, hard-working, likes sports. And he has a mother,' she added, with more feeling in her voice than she had yet shown, something which did not escape her listener.

'In the same town?'

'She has the upstairs apartment in his house. He was born in that house.'

'Ah . . . how long have you known him?'

'Three years.'

'It took him three years to propose?'

How to answer that? Laura neatly dissected her egg. 'Yes, it did.'

'He doesn't deserve you. Are you in love with him?'

Suddenly she had had enough. She looked up, in her eyes the hurt and confusion of three years of being in love, and of an ill-timed proposal. 'Don't badger me, Charles.'

His eyes narrowed. 'There's quite a lot you're not telling me.'

'Of course there is! I've only just met you, for heaven's sake.'

'If you'd rather, we could talk about the weather. They say the temperature's going to seventy-five today. Hottest day so far.'

She was still angry. 'And what about you? Are you married, divorced, or engaged?'

'Nope. Engaged once, four years ago. Broke it off. No serious involvements since.'

'Where are you from?'

'Toronto.' He saw her eyes light up. 'You know it?'

'I grew up there—I love Toronto! What do you do there?'

'I work for a big multi-national corporataion. Mining and industrial interests. I've been on a leave of absence for a while, I have to go back in September.'

Laura was naturally perceptive, a trait that four years of coping with the vagaries of teenagers had sharpened.

There had been a slight evasiveness in Charles's voice; she was instantly reminded of the time Sue-Ann had wanted to go to the school dance and had not wanted to tell Laura she was going with a boy who had been twice suspended for possessing drugs. She said agreeably, 'There's quite a lot you're not telling me, too.'

The grey eyes were disconcertingly sharp. 'No flies on you, Laura. Maybe we should talk about the weather.'

'Maybe we should. Then I'll help you with the dishes and get on my way.'

Half an hour later she was driving away from his cottage. They had discussed a number of innocuous and impersonal subjects; had on the surface, at least, cleaned up the kitchen; and had said goodbye without as much as a handshake, let alone a kiss.

It was a beautiful morning, just as the forecast had predicted. During the two-hour drive to the gas station Laura had plenty of time to think, time she put to good use. You're sex-starved, she berated herself. You've been buried in the country for four long years with Bart your only male interest and three teenagers watching your every move, and now you've met a very attractive man who—be honest, Laura—you'd like to go to bed with. You can't do it. It's not your style. Besides, you're in love with Bart ... aren't you?

But was she? She found herself remembering the last time she had seen Bart, the evening before she had left for Cape Breton. He had not been at all pleased three days earlier when she had told him her plans, and when he picked her up after dinner to go for a drive she knew immediately that he was still annoyed with her, for he had given her a frigid peck on the cheek and had said, 'You upset mother when you implied that we might not be getting married. You told me it was only a matter of time.'

'I told you I needed time to think about it—not quite the same thing.'

'Mother is very fond of you. There's nothing she'd like better than for me to marry you and settle down.'

'In Grantham?' said Laura delicately.

'She'd prefer us to live in Grantham, naturally.'

'Bart, I can't commute back and forth to Halifax every day, it's much too far. And you know I'm planning to re-apply for medical school. When Sue-Ann finishes school next year, I'll be free to do so.'

'I admire your ambition, Laura, don't misunderstand me. But don't you think it's time you faced the facts? You're twenty-five now, not twenty-one. You'd be thirty before you graduated. That's a little old to be embarking on a new career, isn't it?'

'Certainly I would have preferred to be embarking on it right now. But James did die and someone had to look after Darren, Keith and Sue-Ann. So everything's been delayed five years. Thirty isn't altogether over the hill, Bart.'

'So you're going to persist in going to medical school?'

'Of course I am. It's what I want to do. You've always know that.'

'I would have thought marriage might have taken preference,' he said, playing with his moustache with one hand, a sure sign he was angry.

'It doesn't have to be an either-or choice, does it? Can't I have both?'

'I would like us to have children, Laura. Are we to wait until you're well over thirty for that?'

'Lots of people are doing it that way—delaying having a family until their mid-thirties.'

'I don't think that's a wise course of action at all. After all, Laura, there's no necessity for you to earn your living now that you have all that money.'

She felt her nerves tighten. 'Bart, I *want* to be a doctor! Not because of the money. Because it's what I want to do. I thought you understood that.'

'I'm beginning to agree with Mother—that your first duty should be to the home and your family.'

Oh you are, are you? 'I wouldn't be marrying your mother, Bart. I'd be marrying you.'

He gave his moustache a particularly vicious tug, took a deep breath and said in a tone of voice meant to sound conciliatory, 'If the medical profession is that important to you, then I am sure we can work out a compromise. We could move back to Grantham once you've graduated. Or maybe Mother could even move to Halifax. I only want your happiness, Laura.'

They were driving past an apple orchard. Laura said abruptly, 'Let's stop and get out.'

After Bart had parked the car by the side of the road, they walked between two parallel rows of trees, that bore fruit the size of crab-apples. Swallows swooped overhead. Deep in the orchard a pheasant produced its guttural *gronk, gronk,* so unlovely a sound from so handsome a bird. Laura should have felt happy and serene walking hand in hand with the man she loved amid such beauty. But she did not. She felt very much on edge, and had she been alone she would have run as fast and as far she could until the tension was driven from her body and her spirit was at peace.

She glanced up at Bart. He was very good-looking, she thought; Sue-Ann's verdict, that he was a watered-down version of Tom Selleck, was not really fair. He liked skiing and swimming and live theatre, as did she, they had had a lot of good times together. Although she had always known he was close to his mother, she had seen this as a positive rather than a negative side to his character. But before this week he and she had never been discussing marriage, had they? It would not have occurred to her that Mrs Manning might have any input into where and how they lived, nor that Bart would expect her, Laura, to stay home and play house and instantly produce several little Mannings.

The grass swished against her ankles; she listened to the swallows chitter and said, 'I can't give up medical school, Bart. So if that's a genuine barrier for you, then I don't think we can get married.'

'I said we could work something out, Laura.'

'I'd want to feel you were wholeheartedly in favour, not just putting up with a bad situation.'

He drew her into his arms and kissed her. It was a long kiss, more passionate than she was used to. She heard the swallows and the pheasant, felt a branch catch in her hair and the rasp of his moustache, and wondered why she should feel the burgeoning of panic rather than desire.

When he finally raised his head he obviously had not caught her mood. He said in a thick voice, 'Laura, I've never tried to make love to you. The circumstances have never been ideal, have they ? I live in the same house as Mother, and as the only lawyer in town I have a certain reputation to maintain. And you have the two boys and Sue-Ann. But you're very attractive and it hasn't always been easy to hold back. Another reason for us to get married, as I'm sure you'll agree.'

But did she? Or did she harbour the suspicion that her desirability was related to her unexpected acquisiton of wealth? She said quietly, 'There's a lot to consider, Bart. I promise I'll have an answer for you when I come back from Cape Breton.'

'And I'm confident what that answer will be. I know you won't let me down.'

She was not so confident. In silence they had walked back to the car.

Now, as she approached the gas station, Laura found herself remembering Charles's kiss. Charles did not know she had a million dollars. Charles had kissed her because he found her beautiful. And he had been as affected—and as surprised—by that kiss as she had been, she would swear.

The manager of the gas station asked her a couple more questions that would identify the wallet as hers, then passed it over to her. He waved away her sincerely meant offer of a reward, so she filled the gas tank of her Honda at his pumps and ate lunch in the restaurant that made up one side of his building, although the food was not nearly as good as Annie's. Then she set off for the cottage again. The cottage and Charles, she thought with a quiver of anticipation.

However, her first stop was in the mining town of Scots Bay, nearest settlement of any size to the cottage: an untidy sprawl of houses that ranged from a few elegant, architect-designed brick and cedar homes with swimming pools to tiny row houses leaning drunkenly against each other. An aura of dirt and depression hung over the town, for Cape Breton had fallen upon hard times and the knots of unemployed men standing at street corners had become a common sight. The main street had neither trees nor flowers; Laura found the whole place so depressing that she went to the bank, the telephone company and the supermarket as quickly as she could, anxious to get back to the cottage. She was in the parking lot beside the grocery store bundling her purchases into the boot when she saw the one person other then Annie whom she knew in the area—Charles.

She was instantly reminded of the Pied Piper of Hamelin, because he was surrounded by a raggle-taggle band of boys. Teenagers, she judged, about a dozen of them, Sue-Ann's age and younger. They were in high spirits, tossing a basketball back and forth, making a good deal of noise, a ghetto blaster providing the raucous thump of one of Sue-Ann's favourite bands. Charles, looking imperturbable, was the centre of the group, its focus and somehow its controlling force.

They passed out of sight. Thoughtfully Laura locked the boot. She had already sensed there was a great deal more to Charles Richards than met the eye, a suspicion that had just been confirmed. She wanted to know why he was herding that unruly bunch of boys down the main street of a mining town on a hot July afternoon. From Wagner to Twisted Sister ... a man of contradictions.

The cottage welcomed her home. She stashed away the groceries, changed into her bikini and carrying a towel and her organic chemistry text headed for the beach. A hammock, which she had not noticed last night in the dark, was strung between two trees at the edge of the meadow. She loved hammocks. But first she'd have to look at the beach. Charles was in town, she would have it to herself.

And so she did. She saw a long curve of pale grey sand, dotted with purple-veined mussel shells and orange strands of dried kelp, and laved by white foam. Whiter than snow, thought Laura, watching the waves advance and retreat. Whiter than clouds could ever be. And, less poetically, horribly cold.

She retreated up the sand to the hammock, spread her towel over the mesh and carefully lay down on her back. She had not once this summer gone outside to lie in the sun in the backyard at Grantham; if she were home now she would be baking cookies or making jam or bringing in the wash. Feeling almost guilty, she opened the chemistry text. The anti-Markovnikov addition of HBr to alkenes is a well-know example of free-radical addition to multiple bonds, she read. She placed the book face down on her belly. I'm on holiday, she thought drowsily, rocking herself back and forth. Radicals will keep until tomorrow. I've got nothing to do. Only myself to cook supper for. No one clamouring for the car or a shirt that isn't ironed. *Heavenly* . . . Her eyes closed, the shush of the waves a lullaby impossible to resist.

Laura was deeply asleep when Charles came jogging down the path an hour later. He stopped in his tracks when he saw the woman in the hammock. One of her arms was dangling over the side and a book lay open across her body. Stepping closer, he peered at the title. *Organic Chemistry*, by Reinhold, Smith and Beakston, he read. An incredibly complicated-looking molecule straggled across the cover.

Sun and shadow dappled Laura's body. She slept with the total concentration of a child, her lashes dark smudges on her cheeks, her mouth curved a little as if her dreams were pleasant. In one swift glance he took in the firm breasts and narrow hips, the slender length of thigh and curve of ankle, then looked away, as if to stare at the sleeping woman was to invade her privacy.

He could have followed the track across the meadow to the beach to swim, as was his original plan. But he did not. His eyes were dragged back to Laura's face. Sleeping Beauty and Snow White, he thought with a touch of irony that did not help matters at all. So was he the hero, the prince, to waken her with a kiss? And was she the woman he'd been waiting for, the one who would take away the loneliness that had been his constant companion for years?

As if he had said the words out loud, Laura's eyes opened. Still half-asleep, she saw a man's body towering over her, limned with sunlight. With a cry of alarm she tried to push herself upright, forgetting that she was in a hammock. The hammock lurched, the organic chemistry book fell to the ground and Charles grabbed her before she could follow it. 'You scared me,' she gasped, swinging her legs round, feeling beneath her feet the springy carpet of needles, something solid in a world tilted off-centre.

'I didn't mean to.' He released her with a reluctance he did not bother hiding. 'You looked so sweet, fast asleep. I was contemplating casting myself in the role of Prince Charming. Temporarily, that is. Or do you think Beuty and Beast would be more applicable?'

Laura was tongue-tied. The brief touch of his body, the strong clasp of his arms seemed to have burned their way into her skin and imprinted themselves on her brain, paralysing it from thought.

'Don't look so frightened,' Charles added softly. 'I wouldn't hurt you for the world.'

Shying away from the undisguised tenderness in his face, she noticed the obvious. 'Were you going for a swim?'

'Yes. Why don't you join me?'

'Too cold. And I feel too lazy.'

'Then come and watch. I never stay in long.' He stooped and picked up her book. 'You can do a little light reading while you're waiting.'

With a touch of defensiveness Laura said, 'I'm studying for the medical admissions test in the autumn.'

'For medical school, you mean?'

'That's right.' Unconsciously she was holding her breath, waiting for his reaction.

'Good for you!' he said warmly. 'I don't know you very well but I have a feeling you'd make a fine doctor. So you must already have your bachelor's degree?'

'Yes. From the University of Toronto.'

'Honours by any chance?' She nodded. 'Bright as well as beautiful, huh? Will you go back to university this autumn?'

'No. A year from now.' They were walking across the meadow, where the ox-eyed daisies raised white faces to the sun and the sea wind ruffled her hair. 'I've been the guardian of my brother's children for the last four years, you see, ever since he died. Sue-Ann, the youngest, doesn't finish high school until next year.'

'So for four years you've had to put your own plans on hold. That can't have been easy,' Charles said shrewdly.

The wind had come up so that the waves were tumbling on the beach, playful as children. 'It wasn't, always. But I really had no other choice. This is a beautiful beach, isn't it?'

'If you marry this fellow, you'll still go to medical school.' It was a statement rather than a question; yet Laura hesitated a fraction too long and Charles pounced. 'He doesn't want you to go?'

'He'd move to Halifax and I'd go to Dalhousie,' she said quickly.

'But he'd really prefer you to give it up. Laura, don't do it.'

'And what if it were you?' she said boldly. 'What if the woman you wanted to marry was determined to immerse herself for five years in a very demanding

programme of study. Long hours. Not much time
together. Putting off having children. How would *you*
like that? Particularly if the job at the end of the five
years was very nearly as demanding.'

'I'd give her all the encouragement and support that I
could,' he said, his grey eyes steady on her face.
'Because if she was doing what she really wanted to do
she'd be happy, and that happiness would spill over on
to me. Everything else can be worked out. But if one of
the people in a relationship is hemmed in by the
relationship, prevented from fulfilling himself or
herself—then you can forget it. Disastrous.'

'You're speaking with the voice of experience.'

'Yeah.' His eyes moved to the horizon, that knife-
sharp line where sea met sky. 'Not in a male-female
sense. But my father is a very strong-willed man who
needs to control people, me among them. It took me
quite a while to figure out I could only be happy when I
was doing what I wanted to do and not what he wanted
me to do—and that he and I wouldn't develop any real
intimacy until I'd found the role that suited me.'
Restlessly he moved his shoulders, so that the muscles
rippled under the skin. 'So in that sense I speak from
experience. Set people free and they'll come back to
you. Because they want to, not because they have to . . .
now, how about that swim?'

There were to be no more disclosures about his
father, that was plain. Laura no longer had the drugged
feeling that an afternoon sleep had induced in her, and
the sparkling blue water looked deceptively inviting.
'Sure, why not?' she said with an impish grin.

They dropped their towels to the sand and he
grabbed her hand. 'The only way to get in is to run. If
you creep in inch by inch, it's agony. Ready?'

She was laughing helplessly. 'Why did I let myself get
talked into this?'

'Because you can't resist me.' The laughter faded from
his face. 'Can you resist me, Laura?' And his lips met hers,
his arms pulling her close to the whole length of his body.

There was passion in his kiss and a searching for response, a response she gave freely because she could not have done otherwise. Her lips parted. When she felt the dart of his tongue, the pounding of her heart drowned the splash of the waves and the faraway cry of a seagull; and when eventually his mouth left hers she was clutching him unashamedly.

He spoke first. 'Twenty-four hours ago I hadn't even met you,' he said, and managed the semblance of a smile. 'We'd better go for a swim—same effect as a cold shower.'

'I may sink like a stone,' she said shakily.

'I won't let you. Trust me.'

'I do,' she said with exactly the same lightness of tone, as hand in hand they ran down the sand into the curling, foam-flecked waves.

The ice-cold water drove the breath from Laura's body, and had she been on her own she would have turned tail and fled back up the beach. But Charles was dragging her deeper into the sea. She shrieked as a wave lapped at her waist then rose to her armpits; the sea-floor dropped, and suddenly she was swimming, flailing around and kicking with all her might.

'It's not *that* bad!' Charles yelled.

'I think my circulation's stopped.' She hit a wave with the side of her palm, splashing him, then dived into the shimmering, pale turquoise water. The sand on the ocean floor was ridged into its own tiny waves. She picked up a big white shell from the bottom, loving the freedom of weightlessness, the sense of a different world that she could briefly visit but never inhabit. Charles was swimming towards her. She pushed herself off from the sand, body arched, graceful as a mermaid, and burst upwards into the sun. The water was refreshing now rather than paralysing; her body tingled with life.

They played for another ten minutes before running for the beach and the sun-warmed towels. Little goosebumps stood all over Laura's flesh, while her lashes were spiky with moisture and her hair slicked to her scalp. She felt wonderful.

Beginning to rub herself down, she said conversationally, 'I saw you today. In Scots Bay. With a whole group of boys.'

His smile was rueful. 'Were they behaving themselves?'

She put her head to one side. 'They gave me the impression of barely leashed energy. Not sure I'd want to be the one keeping them in order.'

'There are one or two tough guys in that crew. I'm coaching them in basketball over the summer. In fact, we've got a game tomorrow night in the school auditorium with a team from Sydney—why don't you come?'

'I'd love to!'

'Good. I'll pick you up around seven. And now,' his smile was a touch malicious, 'I'd better let you enjoy some of that solitude you were craving.'

She gazed at him in wide-eyed innocence. 'I was wondering when you'd remember that.'

'Providing it's solitude you crave rather than me?' he said hopefully.

She picked up the unread chemistry book. 'How could I crave you when I have this for company?'

'Very easily, I should think.' He sobered. 'Why don't you forget the studying for a few days, Laura, and have a bit of a holiday. You must be tired to have fallen asleep this afternoon.'

She grimaced as she trod gingerly over the shale. 'I didn't sleep very well last night. Too many strange noises.'

'Any time you need my company . . .'

'I'll call,' she said obligingly. 'Except that I can't, because my 'phone won't be connected for two more days . . . Maybe tomorrow evening I'll come to your place before the game, so I can 'phone home. Just to check that everything's okay.'

'Do it this evening if you'd rather.'

Inwardly berating herself for being tempted, she said, 'No, tomorrow'll be fine. Keith—that's the middle one—says I worry too much, and he's right. They'll manage perfectly well without me.'

She sounded as if she was trying to convince herself. Charles smiled to himself and gestured for her to go ahead as they crossed the meadow. When they reached the fork in the path, Laura turned to face him. 'That was fun?' she said spontaneously. 'Thanks.'

'Any time. Seriously, Laura, if you are nervous alone, feel free to come over to my place, won't you?' His smile was crooked. 'You don't have to worry, I'll preserve my perfect-gentleman image. If it kills me.'

Earlier, jokingly, he had said *trust me*. She did trust him. Instinctively, in a way incapable of analysis or explanation, she knew he would do nothing against her will. 'Thank you, Charles,' she said gravely. Standing on tiptoes, she kissed his cheek. 'I'll see you tomorrow.'

He was looking at her in a way no other man had ever looked at her before. Drowning in that look, longing to throw herself into his arms and make love to him under the trees, she clutched her book to her breast and hurried along the path towards the cottage. She did not dare look back to see if he was still watching her.

CHAPTER FOUR

SHORTLY after six the following evening Laura was walking along the winding trail that connected the two cottages, a trail she had discovered earlier in the day when she was out exploring. The birds that tuned up outside her bedroom window in the morning were still singing their hearts out; with the streak of romanticism that no amount of scientific knowledge could dispell Laura hoped they were singing for joy, rather than to establish territorial claims. Joy seemed more appropriate to the warm, golden evening. Joy was what she felt when she saw Charles loading gear into the back of the Jeep. And joy was in her smile when she walked closer and said shyly, 'Hello, Charles.'

He straightened, putting an athletic bag down on the ground. He was wearing jeans and a T-shirt, undistinguished clothes that he wore with distinction. His smile was a match to hers, his kiss deliberate yet thorough. Taking her hand, he guided it to his chest, where she could feel the heavy pounding of his heart. 'See what you do to me?'

Instant intimacy, she thought. An avoidance of all the normal small talk and the barriers that exist between men and women. A reaching for the essentials.

Her eyes searched his face. 'Why Charles? Why me?'

'Maybe we shouldn't analyse it,' he said slowly. 'Maybe we should just be—glad. That we've met. That we'll be next door to each other for a whole month.'

She and Bart had known each other for three years. 'A month isn't very long.'

'Sometimes a day can hold a whole lifetime, Laura.'

Without warning or reason Laura was seized by a sudden, overwhelming terror. Who was this man whose eyes and mouth and hands had laid claim on her?

Whose body drove from her all vestige of caution, whose voice bewitched her? What did she know of him? *Nothing* . . .

She backed away a step, said raggedly, 'May I use your 'phone?' and before he could say anything fled up the stairs, letting the screen door bang shut behind her.

His bedroom was as untidy as it had been the day before, although he had, sketchily, made his bed. She placed a collect call to her number in Grantham, and while she waited for the connection let her eyes wander around the room. A copy of the *Financial Post* lay on the bed, open to the Toronto Stock Exchange quotations, several of which were underlined. So he dabbled in stocks, did Charles. On top of a heap of *New Yorkers* on the bureau was a book called *In Search of Excellence*, for which Laura had read a review. It was about successful American corporations: more business interests. Beside it was a very beautiful leather shaving kit, stamped with gold initials. C.R.T. Her brow wrinkled. What did the T stand for? Then the 'phone started ringing. Sue-Ann answered and blithely accepted the charges.

'Sue-Ann? Laura here. How are you, dear?'

'Fabulous! I had a wonderful date with Steven last night. We went tubing on the river, then a bunch of us went to the Dairy Queen and pigged out and then he drove me home. He's so neat, Laura, I'm just crazy about him. And, yes, Keith was here when we got home and did the heavy chaperon act, you don't have to worry about a thing.'

Laura laughed. She did not really worry about Sue-Ann, who was always crazy about somebody but who had her head set very firmly on her shoulders. 'I'm glad you're having a good time. How's work?'

They chatted for a few minutes, then Keith came on the line. 'Walker's Chaperon Service,' he intoned.

'Send in the bill at the end of the month! Have you made your reservations for Toronto, Keith?'

'Week after next. Tuesday to Thursday.' He

hesitated. 'I asked the housekeeper if she'd stay here while I was gone.'

'Because Darren isn't around very much,' Laura said resignedly.

'He's got a new job at a dairy farm out of town. So his hours are going to be irregular.'

'I'm glad he's got a job. Is he home now?'

'He just started today. He's not back yet. Are you having a good time, Laura?'

Keith obviously did not want her to dwell on Darren. 'Wonderful,' she said, more warmly than she had intended.

He picked up her intonation instantly. 'You're not lonely?'

'Not at all,' she said demurely. 'I'm using the telephone that belongs to the man next door.'

Keith laughed. 'I hope he's tall, dark and handsome.'

'Blond. But the other two apply.'

'I never was very keen on Bart,' said Keith. There was a tiny silence, for he had never expressed this sentiment to her before. He added, 'You don't mind me saying that, do you?'

'No. I guess not. I—I don't think I'll be marrying him, Keith.'

'Good. It was a bit too slick, him proposing right after you won the lottery.'

So she had not been the only one to notice that. 'I thought I was just being nasty-minded.'

'No way. If anything you're far too trusting. What's this blond fellow's name?'

'Charles Richards,' she said slowly, her eyes resting again on the elegant leather kit with its three gold initials.

'You deserve a bit of a fling, Laura,' Keith said, as if he were her uncle rather than her nephew. 'Want to talk to Sue-Ann again?'

'No, that's all right. I just wanted to check that everything's okay.'

'I'll have to call you as soon as I know the

Toronto results. You gave us your number, didn't you?'

'Yes. The 'phone will be connected tomorrow. I'll be talking to you again before you go—but good luck with Besicaglia.'

'Thanks. I'll need it! More than you'll need Walker's Chaperon Service—right?'

'Goodbye, Keith,' she said firmly, her eyes full of laughter, and put down the 'phone.

Silence in the rest of the cottage; Charles was presumably still outside. She walked over to the bureau and traced the indented gold letters with her fingertip. She might have rationalised the extra initial by assuming the kit was a hand-me-down from an uncle or maternal grandfather if the kit had not been brand new. Was Charles not telling her the truth about something as basic as his name? And if not, why not?

Quickly she flipped open the cover of *In Search of Excellence* but there was no name written inside. The magazines had been purchased at a newsstand rather than being part of a subscription. No clues there. Then the screen door banged, and guiltily Laura hurried around the foot of the bed.

Said Charles casually as she came back into the living room, 'Everything all right?'

For a split second she debated asking him point-blank about the initials on the shaving kit. But that would indicate she had been poking around in his belongings, and she shrank from such an admission. There had to be a simple explanation, something very obvious. Charles would not lie to her. She gave him a quick smile. 'Fine. Sue-Ann's in love, and Keith's going to Toronto in two weeks for his auditions.' A faint shadow crossed her face. 'Darren wasn't home.'

Charles glanced at his watch. 'We'd better go, I have to get there early. On the way there why don't you tell me about them, Laura? Where did you say you lived?'

She hadn't said. She smiled vaguely. 'One of the little towns in the Annapolis Valley. Orchards, tobacco farms and livestock. I suffered from severe culture shock when I moved there after four years at the University of Toronto . . . I won't need a sweater, will I?'

'No. The gym's usually too warm if anything.'

As they got in the Jeep and drove away, she began telling him about Sue-Ann, Keith and Darren, rather pleased with herself that she had avoided mentioning Grantham by name. She had a deep, irrational fear of letting him know where she lived. What if he went there? He would immediately find out about her newly won wealth and everything would change.

Thinking about money reminded Laura of something else. She took out her wallet and counted out the exact amount of her bill at Annie's two days before, adding some change for the tip. 'This is the money I owe you for my dinner,' she said.

Charles glanced down at the the collection of bills and coins in her hand and looked acutely uncomfortable. 'Put that away, Laura.'

'No!' she retorted spiritedly. 'I owe you this money, Charles.'

'Please—I was abominably rude to you that evening, don't rub my nose in it.'

She glared at him. 'You apologised for your rudeness and I accepted that apology. The money is a separate issue altogether. I'm going to sit here until you take it, so you might as well give in gracefully.'

He gave her a sideways look full of mockery. 'I can see your patients will have to behave themselves. Dr Walker on the rampage will be a terrifying sight.'

'*You* don't look exactly terrified.'

'I'm not,' he said mildly. 'But I will take the money. I can see it's important to you.'

'But do you understand why?' she asked anxiously.

They had pulled up at a traffic light on the outskirts of the town. Charles took the money from her and shoved it in the back pocket of his jeans. 'Yes. Sure I do. One pays one's debts—a point of honour. Which is not a word that's in fashion, but I seem to be stuck with it. As do you.'

She was glad he understood, all the more so because he had had her worried for a minute or two. She said with something of his own sly mockery, 'Glad that's settled. It's very bad strategy for a woman to be indebted to a man.'

'Now that *is* a separate issue,' he chuckled. 'Not that you need to worry. You're well able to look after yourself, indebted or not.' He drew up by the kerb. 'This is as near as we can get.'

People were trickling into the gymnasium as they arrived. Charles disappeared and Laura picked out a good seat on the bleachers, content to watch the comings and goings. The audience was largely teenagers, the boys leather-jacketed, the girls heavily made-up. Their conversation was unsubtle, their energy raw, with an undercurrent of aggression that Laura could understand, given the economic conditions, but could also deplore. The adults of tomorrow, she mused, watching a burly town policeman break up a tussle by the door; would they make a better job of the world or would they be as powerless as any other generation to halt the forces of greed and the misuse of power?

As the team ran out on the court to warm up, she abandoned her somewhat depressing train of thought. The boys from Sydney in their glossy green uniforms were larger and more assured than Charles's team, whose dull-coloured T-shirts and unmatched socks gave them the scruffy look of a flock of winter sparrows. Charles had told her on the way in that he did not expect them to win, for they had only been together as a team for a month and half. 'But they'll put up a good fight,' he said. And he was right.

Two of his forwards were natural players, one a rangy black boy who moved with a fluid grace, the other a scrappy little redhead who darted in between the other players like a weasel in a chicken-run. However, their defensive play was weak and they lost points on foul shots, of which there were many, for the game was rough enough that the referee was kept busy. At half time the Sydney team was ahead by eight points. With three minutes left in the game the redhead tied the score at seventy-all. But within seconds the Sydney centre, who stood six-feet-five, scored two baskets, and the final score was eighty-two to seventy-four.

Laura clapped with the rest, afterwards watching Charles gather his team around him. Although she could not hear what he was saying, she could gauge his intensity; she saw the redhead's dispirited shoulders lift a little, heard the team break into laughter, watched them run off the court to the dressing rooms with a new energy. From the floor Charles waved at her. She climbed down the bleachers and said sincerely, 'That was an exciting game. You've done wonders if they've only been together for six weeks.'

'Thanks.' He was sweating, his grin so boyish that she was touched. 'I'll be a few more minutes, I have to help lock up.'

'I'll wait outside—it's really warm in here.'

'Okay. Won't be long.'

He jogged away from her over the polished hardwood floor. As she walked towards the exit Laura knew she had learned a lot about Charles this evening, things that made the extra initial on the shaving kit seem trivial. He cared about the ten boys on his team. His concentration had been absolute throughout the entire game and he had got the very best out of his motley collection of players. The players, in turn, respected him; she had the feeling it would not be easy to gain the respect of sixteen- and seventeen-year-olds in a mining town in Cape Breton.

Outside the air was a little cooler and the crowd dispersing. She wandered down the pavement and sat down near the parked Jeep on a stone wall, behind which an alleyway between two buildings disappeared into the darkness. The stores were all closed. She could see a crowd of teenagers clustered around a dairy bar at the far end of the street, thought of Sue-Ann and Steven, and smiled to herself.

From behind her came a scuffle of footsteps, the thud of blows and a broken-off cry. The smile was wiped from her face. Her heart began to pound. She stood up, peering down the dark alleyway, barely able to discern three struggling figures. Two on top, one underneath. Another muffled shout and the sickening crunch of fist on flesh.

Ever since childhood when she had inadvertently been a witness to a mugging Laura had had a horror of physical violence. Not stopping to think, adrenalin pouring through her veins, she let out a blood-curdling scream for help and ran down the alley, swinging her bag, which was never light at the best of times, by its strap. 'You stop that!' she yelled, aiming for the nearest assailant's head with her bag and letting out another banshee screech. She heard a string of oaths that ordinarily would have made her hair curl but now only served to make her angrier; her handbag connected with some portion of the other attacker's anatomy with a most satisfying thump. The boy underneath managed to land a kick. Then a flashlight shone into the alley and a deep male voice demanded, 'What's going on here?'

The two attackers did not stay around to answer. Staggering upright, they took off in the opposite direction, the second catching Laura unawares with one last vicious swipe of his arm that almost knocked her off her feet. She hit the brick wall with her elbow and yelped at the sudden pain.

'Laura! Are you all right? Those bastards——'

It was Charles, outstripping the burly policeman and his flashlight by several feet. She grabbed his sleeve, for he looked capable of murder. 'Kid on the ground,' she gasped, cradling her elbow. 'See if he's hurt.'

The beam of the flashlight showed a boy of perhaps

fifteen in a torn checked shirt and dirty jeans. He was half crouching, clutching his lower body, his face contorted with pain. The policeman knelt down and said with rough sympathy, 'It's okay, Johnny—you'll feel better in a minute. You okay, miss?'

'I'm fine,' Laura said, which was near enough to the truth. 'I don't know why they call it your funny bone,' she muttered in an aside to Charles. 'Nothing funny about it.'

'Are you hurt anywhere else?' he rapped.

'Don't think so . . . will he be all right?'

'He got kicked where it hurts,' Charles said harshly. 'Those guys weren't playing parlour games, Laura— they were fighting dirty.' When he took her in his arms he discovered she was trembling from reaction. His grip tightened. 'They were twice your size, for God's sake— didn't you even stop to think?'

'I didn't realise how big they were until they stood up.' The trembling was getting worse; she felt sick. Burrowing her face into his shoulder she stuttered, 'Are you trying to tell me I should have minded my own business?'

'I guess not. What I'm trying to say is thank God you weren't seriously hurt.'

A small crowd had gathered at the entrance of the alleyway. They're all there now we don't need them, thought Laura fuzzily. She said. 'I could do with a good stiff drink.'

'You shall have one as soon as we get home,' Charles replied, a thread of laughter in his voice. 'I even bought some gin today with you in mind. Although I didn't realise we'd be drinking it under quite such drastic circumstances.'

The policeman cleared his throat self-importantly. 'I'll have to ask you to come to the station to make a statement, miss.'

'We'll follow you,' Charles said briefly. 'What about Johnny?'

Johnny by now was upright, revealing himself to be

skinny, not very tall and far from clean. He shrilled, 'I ain't telling you who done it. They'll have it in for me if I tell.'

Beneath Johnny's surface belligerence Laura could see genuine, and no doubt justified, fear. When the policeman asked, 'Can you describe the assailants, miss?' she answered with just the right touch of bewilderment, 'Not really. It was dark, you see, and I was trying to stop them, not describe them. One of them might have had black hair and one brown. Although I wouldn't swear to it. They were both wearing black leather jackets, I did notice that.'

'So's half the rest of the town,' said the policeman dourly. 'Couldn't you see their faces?'

'Well, no. I was behind them the whole time.'

The policeman took out his notebook, wrote down her name and the address of the cottage, said even more dourly, 'Not much sense in you coming to the station then,' and turned back to Johnny. 'Come on, young fellow. I'll run you home. Your mum home?'

'Dunno,' Johnny said. He seemed to be rapidly recovering what Laura guessed was a naturally happy-go-lucky disposition. He gave Laura a cheeky grin and a thumbs-up signal. 'Thanks a lot. Do the same for you some day.'

'I hope you won't have to,' she rejoined. 'Stay out of dark alleys, huh?'

He gave her another cheeky grin as he trotted out behind the policeman. Charles said in an undertone, 'You could have described the other two, couldn't you?'

'Yes. Particularly the one who hit me.'

'Good thing you weren't put under oath at the police station.'

'The policeman knew I could describe them. But he also heard what Johnny said. That's the way small towns operate, Charles.'

'I wondered as much. I don't want you walking the streets of Scots Bay at night, Laura. Because if you can describe them, they can no doubt recognise you. Do you hear me?'

'Yes,' she said meekly. 'Can we go home now?'

'Can't wait for that gin?'

She was utterly exhausted, with aches and pains making themselves known in various parts of her body. But she was not going to tell him that. 'That's right,' she agreed. 'But if you were to offer me your arm I wouldn't refuse it.'

'What the hell am I going to do with you, Laura?' he said in exasperation.

'Take me home.'

'That's not what I meant and you know it. You did a very brave thing this evening—I'm proud of you.'

Tears pricked at her eyes. 'Thank you,' she quavered. 'Now please take me home before I start to howl like a baby.'

Solemnly he held out his arm. She took it, feeling the roughness of hair and the heat of his skin under her fingers. Avoiding the inquisitive stares of the people still clustered at the entrance to the alley, she watched Johnny drive away in the front seat of the police car. Then Charles helped her into the Jeep. She leaned back in the seat with a sigh of relief and closed her eyes.

She didn't remember much about the drive home; maybe she slept. She surfaced when Charles turned off the road on to the gravelled road that led to the cottages, and mumbled, 'I think we'll forget about the gin. I need to go to bed.'

He took the left-hand fork without comment, and when he had parked beside her cottage, opened the door on her side. She slid to the ground, biting off an exclamation of pain as her weight landed on her right ankle.

'What's wrong?' Charles said sharply.

'I think one of them must have landed a kick on my shin. Don't look like that, Charles—I'll survive.'

'I'm coming in with you. Where's the key?'

'Why are you angry with me?' she cried.

His face gentled. 'Laura dear, I'm not angry with *you*. I'd like to have those two guys here right now so I could land a few good kicks of my own.'

'Oh,' she said faintly. 'I see.'

'I blame myself—I should never have let you wait for me outside.'

'You didn't know what was going to happen.'

'I could have guessed.'

'Charles, you're not God.'

Some of the strain eased from his face. 'It's not a role I aspire to.'

'Then don't blame yourself when you're not all-seeing.'

'You're telling me off, aren't you?'

'Yes, I believe I am.'

'You're good for me, Laura,' he said abruptly. 'You treat me like——' He broke off.

Her ankle was hurting atrociously and she was longing to lie down, but it seemed more important that Charles finish his statement. 'Like what?'

'I was going to say like an ordinary person.'

'Well, aren't you an ordinary person?'

'I—I can't really answer that. I told you a bit about my father ... circumstances haven't always been ordinary.' He made another sudden shift in the conversation. 'You look like you're going to pass out.'

'It's an option,' she returned with a tiny smile. 'The key's somewhere in my bag.'

He found it in a commendably short time, said, 'Stay there,' unlocked the door, then came back and picked her up. She put her arms around his neck and let her cheek rest against his shoulder. 'You're being very masterful,' she murmured. Although Keith, fooling around, had carried her around the house over his shoulder one day, no one had ever held her in his arms with such a paradoxical mixture of strength and gentleness. She discovered that she liked it. Very much.

'Which room is yours?'

'The far door.'

He pushed open the door with his foot, walked into the room and put her down on the bed. 'There's not much to you,' he commented.

'One hundred and twenty pounds!' she said indignantly.

'We must never have a serious fight. Because it's obvious who'd win.'

'You're far too complex a man to use brute force, Charles,' she answered, batting her lashes at him.

He was not impressed. 'Roll up your trouser leg. I want to see the damage to your shin.'

The cuffs of her trousers were fashionably narrow at the ankle. 'I can't roll them up, they're too tight.'

He looked down at her ankles and said, 'Then get into your nightclothes. I'll be the perfect gentleman but I want to see what those guys did to you.'

'Charles, I won't fall apart if I've got a few bruises.'

'Laura, do as you're told.

'You sound horribly parental!'

'I don't feel the slightest bit parental. Now will you please do what I say?'

'Or you'll pit your two hundred pounds against my one hundred and twenty—is that it?' she said nastily.

He looked every bit as angry as she. 'Yeah . . . that could be it. I've never known such an independent, argumentative, bloody-minded woman as you!'

'So do you prefer women who do exactly as you say the minute you say it?' she blazed. 'If so, you've got the the wrong woman, Charles Richards!'

'I'm going out of this room, Laura, and I'm coming back in exactly five minutes, at which time you can show me the bruise on your shin and I shall then leave. Is that clear?'

'If I get into my nightdress it's because I want to, not because you're telling me to!'

'. . . and I'm not at all sure you're the wrong woman,' he added with a sardonic lift of his brow as he went out of the room and very quietly closed the door behind him.

Laura used a word that Darren would have recognised, a very short, earthy word that expressed her feelings exactly. Then she rummaged under the pillow for her nightdress and limped over to the wardrobe for her robe. They were pretty garments, knee-length, of flowered cotton decorated with lace and ribbon; vindictively she wished that her lifestyle had been such that they were French silk, slinky, seductive, and sophisticated. She'd like Charles to suffer a bit. To have to struggle to maintain his pose of a perfect gentleman. Angrily she hauled off her shirt and bra, throwing them on the chair, then pulled the offending nightdress over her head. Sandals, trousers and bikini briefs followed the rest of her clothes. Only then, dismayed, did she look down at her legs.

As she knew from her biochemistry courses, in emergencies adrenalin flooded the system with glucose for fight-or-flight behaviour; a side effect was obviously the masking of pain. In the fracas in the alley she had been kicked more than once, for there were several pinkish swellings between her knees and her ankles, and even some skin scraped off the shin bone. The pink would turn to purple then to yellow, in the manner of bruises. She was going to look beautiful in shorts, she thought wretchedly. *Oh damn* . . .

A tap at the door. She grabbed for her robe as Charles walked in. She might privately have bemoaned the wholesomeness of her nightgown, but as she stood by the bed, shoulders and arms bare, with the bedside light shining through the thin fabric, it was obvious that the effect on Charles was all she could have wished.

She snapped, 'A perfect gentleman would have waited until asked to come in.' Then in faint horror she recognised the shrewishness in her voice and stammered, 'Charles, I'm sorry. Why are we fighting like this?'

He deliberately stayed by the door. 'Sexual frustration, I would think. Wouldn't you?'

Her mouth dropped open, the robe dangling

forgotten in her hand. Stammering even worse, she said, 'But I don't . . . but we can't . . .'

'We don't have to do anything about it, Laura. But we might as well acknowledge that it's there.'

She sat down on the edge of the bed, absently pulling on the gown, and announced, 'I've never slept with Bart.'

'Another reason not to marry him,' Charles said promptly. 'If you can keep your hands off each other for three years, that doesn't say much for passion, does it?'

'I had an affair in college.'

'True confessions, Laura?'

'There hasn't been anyone since.'

There was defiance in her abrupt little pronouncements. Charles hesitated, still carefully standing by the door. 'Did you enjoy the affair?'

'Not terribly. I mean, it was okay.' Her grimace was endearing. 'Not quite what *Sonnets from the Portuguese* had led me to expect.'

'Perhaps that's why you haven't had another?'

'That, and a minor detail like three teenagers underfoot twenty-four hours a day, seven days a week for the past four years.'

'As we seem to be into baring our souls, allow me to say that while there's nothing I'd like better than to take you to bed right now, I'm not going to do so.' His mouth twisted. 'Sounds arrogant as hell, doesn't it, because I'm going on the assumption you'd be willing. Even if you were, I still wouldn't. Not right now. Not yet. And don't ask me to explain that, because I can't.' He must have caught the flicker of uncertainty in her eye. 'It's not because I don't want you. Don't ever think that.'

'Oh.' She looked down at the floor and said unnecessarily, 'I do a lot of blushing when you're around.'

'That, too, flatters me. Now, show me your ankle.'

Wordlessly she lifted both legs. He knelt beside her,

his hands encircling her ankles. 'God, Laura—they must have been wearing steel-toed boots.'

'I honestly didn't feel a thing.'

He looked up at her, his expression so full of concern that she had to will herself not to throw her arms around his neck and pull him back on the bed.

Something of this must have shown in her face. He dropped her ankles as if they were burning his hands, got to his feet and said roughly, 'So much for good intentions. I'd better get out of here . . . put some cold water on those bruises, it'll help the swelling go down. I'll drop over tomorrow morning to see how you're feeling. Good night.'

'Good night, Charles.'

He was gripping the door frame, and she sensed the effort he was making to sound natural. 'I wish to God your 'phone was connected. I don't like the thought of you over here alone—particularly tonight.'

How easy it would be to ask him to sleep in the other room. He would do so, if she asked. She knew he would. 'I'll be fine,' she said steadily, dredging up a smile. 'I never have nightmares and I'm tired enough to sleep the clock round.'

'You know where I am if you need me.' His eyes trained on her face, he added, 'Before the month is over, we'll have to resolve this somehow, Laura.'

By going to bed? By falling in love? Or both? 'I suppose we will,' she said in a small voice. And until we do, I'm not going to tell you that I'm worth a million dollars.

'See you tomorrow.' As if there was nothing else to say, he gave a salute of his hand and was gone. She heard him cross the living room and shut the door behind him. I should get up and lock it, she thought hazily. But it's a long way to walk. So she didn't.

CHAPTER FIVE

LAURA slept through the hours of darkness, through the sun's slow climb over the horizon, through the chorus of birdsong. She slept past the time she would normally be getting Sue-Ann off to school, and the time she herself would be arriving at work. She slept through the knock on the outside door and the fall of footsteps towards her bedroom door.

Charles stood in the doorway, exactly where he had stood twelve hours earlier. A dark head was burrowed into the pillow. A slim arm lay over the covers, fingers loosely curled. He could hear the quiet rhythm of her breathing.

In the living room the telephone rang. The bell was turned to its loudest pitch. Laura woke with a start, heard the second shrill ring and saw Charles in the same instant. Still half asleep she sat up, stifling a groan at her sore muscles, and swung her legs to the floor. The 'phone rang for the third time.

She scurried past Charles, who was still standing unhelpfully in the doorway, reached the telephone and picked up the receiver before that ear-splitting bell could ring again. 'Hello?'

'Telephone company, ma'am,' said a woman's nasal voice. 'Your telephone has been connected. You'll be billed from this date, along with the service charge. Address any queries to the business office. Thank you and have a good day.'

The connection was cut. Said Laura, into the dial tone, 'You, too,' and put down the receiver.

She ached in every limb. Glancing down at her legs, she saw purple-edged shadows where the swellings had been. Her ribs were sore where she had crashed into the wall. Her elbow hurt. She said distinctly, 'Charles, if you like me at all, you'll put the kettle on and make me a cup of very strong black coffee.'

'Glad to oblige,' he said lazily. 'Once you've kissed me good morning.'

He was barefoot, in cut-off shorts and a skin-tight singlet. Her nightgown if not slinky and sophisticated was certainly brief. 'I don't think that's such a good idea.'

'Come on, Laura, where's your sense of adventure? Anyone who ventures into dark alleyways can't be afraid of a kiss.'

'Oh yes, I can,' she said warmly. 'What happens to me in dark alleyways is a lot less dangerous than what happens when I come within ten feet of you.'

'As I believe I've said before, you're marvellously good for the ego. One kiss. That's all.'

Laura had never been good at turning down challenges. 'Coffee first, then the kiss?' she suggested.

'No. I prefer my order of events.'

'Very well, then,' she said composedly. 'Good morning, Charles,' and lifted her face, closing her eyes.

Her hearing was normally acute. But he approached her soundlessly. She felt hands move slowly up her arms from wrist to shoulder, where they lingered, massaging her flesh. Eyes squeezed shut, she said, 'That's not kissing.'

'The prelude,' he said, his breath stirring her hair. 'If I'm only to get one, I want it to last. Relax, Laura.'

How could she, when all her senses were clamouring for his touch? His palms were sliding down her back, drawing her hips close to his; against her breasts she felt the hard wall of his chest and wondered if he could hear the frantic thudding of her heart.

He had been in control until then. But the moment his mouth found hers his control broke. He strained her to him, his hands frantically moving over her body as if to learn its every curve and thereby imprint the softness of her flesh upon his brain. His kiss was deep, speaking of a passionate hunger.

Shaken to the core Laura clung to him, her own
hunger as shockingly obvious as his. She scarcely
recognised the first shrill ring of the telephone, so lost
was she in the sensations of her own body. But then it
pealed again Charles loosened his hold on her. Their
lips parted. Totally disorientated, Laura rushed over to
the wall. 'Hello?' she croaked.

'Sorry to bother you, ma'am. It's the telephone
company again. I forgot to ask you if you needed a new
directory.'

Her head whirling, Laura gasped. 'Oh. No—thanks. I
already have one.'

'You're welcome. Have a nice day.'

Laura put the receiver back on the hook and pushed
the lever to reduce the volume of the bell. Then she
leaned against the wall and looked at Charles. His hair
was ruffled, his grey eyes ablaze; she could think of
nothing to say that sounded neither trite nor flip, so
wisely remained silent.

'We've resolved one thing, haven't we?' he said
heavily. 'We want to make love to each other. I want
you in my bed, Laura. Now.'

'We scarcely know each other.'

'Maybe that doesn't matter. Maybe that will all fall
into place.'

She was hugging her arms to her breast. 'I don't
know,' she said helplessly. 'I came up here thinking I
was in love with someone else. And here I am just
about in bed with you.'

'I don't think you're in love with him at all.'

'That doesn't say much for my emotional judgment—
or stability.'

'Don't be so hard on yourself. We all make mistakes.
Just be glad you didn't marry him.'

She shivered. 'I'm going to get dressed. What about
that coffee I was promised?'

'I've put too much pressure on you, haven't I?' She
nodded miserably, not looking at him. 'I'm sorry ...
Don't push the river, it'll flow by itself—there's a book

by that title, isn't there? The time will come when it will
seem right for us to make love, Laura. I know it will.'

Laura, who during the years in Grantham had
cultivated an evenness of temper, almost a placidity,
now felt like throwing the telephone directory at the
wall or else indulging in a good cry. Or both. 'When
I've had my shower,' she muttered, 'I'll expect the
coffee to be made.'

'Did you hear what I said?'

There was an inflexible note to his voice. 'Yes, I
heard,' she said wildly. 'But I have no idea what to
reply. So I'm going to have a shower—okay?' And with
as much dignity as she could muster in her lace-
bedecked nightgown she stalked past him. He did not
attempt to stop her.

A shower restored much of Laura's equanimity. She
dressed in jeans and a long-sleeved shirt, and went into
the kitchen with her hair still curling damply around
her ears. Accepting a mug of steaming coffee, she said
gratefully, 'Thanks, Charles.'

'I wanted to make you some toast but I couldn't find
the bread.'

'Oh, it's in the cupboard over here.' She put her
coffee on the counter and opened the corner cupboard,
bending to the back shelf for the bread. As she reached
for the plastic bag, she saw movement. A tiny grey body
scuttled along the shelf, found itself trapped in the
corner and darted back towards her hand. A mouse.

Dropping the bag as if it were alive, Laura screamed,
backed up, banged her head on the counter and landed
in a heap on the floor.

'Laura——'

'There's a mouse in the cupboard!' she babbled,
scrambling to her feet. 'I'm terrified of them. Do
something, Charles.'

But rather than rushing to the rescue he began to
laugh, the helpless, infectious laughter of true amusement. '*Charles*!' she sputtered. But the sight of her
furious face only made him laugh all the harder. She

grabbed her coffee mug from the counter and retreated to the far corner of the room. 'I'm glad you think it's funny,' she said coldly.

He was wiping his eyes, his chest still shaking with laughter. 'You'll take on a couple of thugs without batting an eye, but a mouse a fraction your size has you terrorised. Don't you know you're supposed to jump on top of a chair? And surely you can scream louder than you did? Oh Laura, I've caught you out—for once you've behaved like a typical female.'

'Now you can act like Sir Galahad and St George the Dragon-Slayer rolled into one and get rid of that damned mouse. And don't you dare start laughing again!'

He crouched down and peered into the cupboard, moving a few things on the shelves. 'I think it's gone.'

'I bet it's just hiding,' she said bitterly. 'Waiting for me.'

'I could set a trap.'

'I hate traps, they seem so cruel. And anyway, then I get left with the body.'

'Well, I could put down some poison.'

She made a face. 'Doesn't that make them swell up and burst?'

'I've got a 308 in the cabin,' he said blandly.

'A 308?'

'A rifle, Laura.'

Glowering, she retorted, 'All I want you to do is pick up the mouse by the tail and put it outside.'

'So it can crawl right back in again.'

'I suppose you're right.' She sighed. 'One way to diet—I'll be scared to death to open the food cupboard. Did it get into the bread?'

Charles pulled the loaf from the shelf. 'No. Want some toast?'

'Please.'

They ate toast and jam at the table by the window. Fog had rolled in during the night, constricting the view to a circle of trees and wet grass with the occasional seagull drifting across their field of vision. The sound of the sea was muffled; the air was still.

As Charles drained his coffee, he said, 'A good day to get some work done. I've been letting it pile up. Why don't we cook supper together, Laura? Would you like to do that?'

She would. 'Your place or mine?'

'Mine. No mice. I'll have to go into town later on to mail some letters, I'll pick up a couple of steaks.' He pushed back his chair. 'Don't study too hard, will you?' Leaning forward, he kissed her chastely on the cheek and let himself out.

For several minutes Laura sat by the window staring sightlessly at the black, drenched trees. Then with a sigh she blanked Charles from her mind, fetched the organic chemistry text and concentrated on the complexities of alkyl halides instead.

She had always been blessed with the ability to concentrate. Four chapters and three hours later she realised she was hungry. She made herself a sandwich and munched on it standing by the window, then decided to go for a walk; the soft, pearl-grey light was oddly appealing. After pulling on rubber boots and a windbreaker she went outside.

The mist had intensified the scent of resin from the evergreens and the cold tang of the sea. When she brushed against a spruce bough, Laura caused a miniature rainfall; in the meadow tiny drops of water clung to the grass like transparent seeds. The rocks on the shore glowed in a multiplicity of colours: rose pink, turquoise and green. The cottage had vanished. The horizon did not exist.

Laura walked on slowly, hands in her pockets, her boots leaving a trail of footprints in the narrow band of grey sand above the high water mark, for the tide was beginning its slow retreat. Then she stopped, staring downwards. Another set of prints had joined her own, these cloven-hoofed, dug deeply into the sand. Deer tracks. Fresh deer tracks, going in the same direction as she.

She peered ahead of her, straining eyes and ears. But all she saw was the greyness of mist and the blurred rocks, and to her ears came only the croak of a raven and the splash of the waves. She walked faster, no longer alone in the fog, certain that any moment she would see a brown flank, a velvet eye, the flick of a white tail.

The tracks meandered along, following the curve of the beach. Then a few hundred yards before the headland they vanished. The deer had taken to the rocks.

When Laura climbed up the bank of shale she could see the trail across the meadow where the deer had brushed moisture from the green blades of grass; she followed it until it disappeared into the tangled alders and the swamp.

Very slowly she began to retrace her steps, still filled with a sense of wonder engendered by that other, shadowy presence, seen yet unseen. She walked back along the sand, adding a third set of prints, and knew she was going straight to Charles's cottage to tell him what had happened. He would understand that illusive closeness to another creature and another world.

When she reached his cottage, she tapped on the screen door. She could hear his voice through the mesh, because the other door was open, and realised he was speaking on the 'phone. He had not heard her knock.

She hesitated, not wanting to eavesdrop, wondering if she should come back in a few minutes. Yet even as she wavered, she was noticing how strangely unlike himself he sounded. This man was speaking in a clipped, authoritarian voice, ramming his points home, scarcely allowing the other person to speak. 'I don't give a damn what Patson wants. He blew it when he undersold the Madson portfolio—two and a half million, for God's sake. Did he think we wouldn't pick up on that?' A brief silence. 'Patson's out, I said. Do you hear? *Out*. No further discussion. What we've got to do is consolidate those shares, even if we have to sell some of

Atco to do it.' Another charged silence. 'Four million isn't too high . . .'

He had appeared in the bedroom doorway, holding the receiver in one hand, the base of the telephone in the other, jabbing the air with it as he talked. He saw Laura immediately and broke off in mid-sentence.

They were twenty feet apart, yet she felt the force of his anger like a physical blow. He covered the receiver with his hand. 'What the hell are you doing here?'

In a small, clear voice she said, 'I knocked, but you didn't hear me.'

'How long have you been standing there?'

'Only a couple of minutes. Charles, I——'

Furiously he interrupted her. 'Don't you know better than to listen to private conversations?'

'I wasn't——'

'What I'm discussing is highly confidential. For God's sake, Laura, I expected better of you——'

'I wasn't *spying*!'

He ignored her frantic denial, his eyes as hard as the stones on the beach. 'Get out of here—I can't talk to you now. You'll have to come back later.' And he turned his back on her.

She felt physically ill. She stumbled down the steps, her only desire to put as much distance as possible between her and the man on the telephone, a man who had flayed her with eyes and voice and left her sick and shivering.

She ran down the path to the beach and pounded along the ridge, rocks clattering down the slope in her wake. The deer tracks were still imprinted in the sand. She saw them now as the tracks of a creature doomed, for how could the deer co-exist with humanity? It would be shot by hunters or chased to exhaustion by dogs or hit by a car. We are destroyers, she thought numbly. We ruin what we touch.

She had a stitch in her side. Slowing down, she saw she had reached the headland, where a promontory of rocks speared its way into the sea and the waters sucked and gurgled. She climbed out on the rocks and sat down, hunched over, her chin on her hands. The rocks had been worn smooth by the ceaseless barrage of the sea; strands of seaweed undulated with the surge of the tide like the hair of a drowned woman.

Laura sat for a long time, until her nerves had calmed and her deep, inner trembling had stilled. Then, finally, she began to think. Charles is a stranger to me. A total stranger. I thought I knew him, but I don't. He turned on me like a savage . . . and I don't know why.

Now that she was allowing the questions to surface, the unease in her mind grew. On her fingers she could tick off all the blanks in her knowledge of him. He had mentioned a father. But what of a mother, brothers and sisters? Why had his engagement been broken? Where had he grown up? What kind of a business was he in that would give him a leave of absence? And why had he been angry out of all proportion when she had overheard a conversation about that business? The amounts of money he had named had been large . . . but did that justify his reaction?

With a sickening lurch of her heart she wondered if he was engaged in something illegal. Backroom deals not mentioned in the annual reports, transactions hidden from the shareholders and the tax officials.

Not Charles, she thought desperately. Please God, not Charles. Yet such a conclusion would explain what she otherwise found inexplicable.

She sat until her hair was dewed with moisture and the chill had penetrated her clothes. Then she walked back the length of the beach. She had arrived at one conclusion: she did not want to see Charles again today. The last thing she wanted was a cosy supper *à deux* at his cottage. He could eat both steaks himself. She hoped he'd choke on them.

She approached her cottage with care, half afraid that he might be waiting for her. But there was no sign of him. She hurried inside, changed into dry jeans and another jacket, grabbed a paperback novel and her bag,

and left again. Backing the car around, she drove to the
highway and turned left.

The fog still cast its pall over land and sea. The road
wound along the coast past lonely stretches of scrub
spruce, rocky beaches, and tiny fishing villages where
the houses clung to the rocks and the lobster traps were
heaped on the wharves. It was a harsh land, and
ungenerous; food could be wrested from the soil and
fish from the sea only by hard, unrelenting toil, in much
the same way now as it had been for three hundred
years.

The places names were a mixture of English and
French, for the mighty fortress of Louisbourg, built in
the reign of Louis XV, had reared its ramparts and iron
cannon only a few miles down the coast. Laura knew
that part of the fortress had been meticulously
reconstructed on the original site, and during the
summer months was peopled with guards, noblemen,
maids and fishermen in costumes of the period. She
wanted to go to Louisbourg; but not today.

At Catalone Gut she sat by the shore watching the
sandpipers dart among the rocks. A great blue heron
flapped silently through the mist, alighted on the sand
flats and poised itself, motionless, in the shallow water.
Dusk fell, the grey of fog becoming the grey of evening.
Ever since Charles's eyes, inimical, cold with anger, had
driven Laura from his door, she had been feeling as
sore in spirit as in body; now the slow, serene rhythms
of nature gave her back a measure of peace. It was
nearly dark when she got up from the rock, scattering a
flock of sandpipers, and headed back to the car.

Although she was hungry, she was not hungry
enough to go back to the cottage and cook a solitary
meal. Annie with her orange curls and booming voice
was just the antidote she needed. She would go to
Annie's for a late dinner.

When she reached the restaurant Laura scanned the
parking area for a grey and black Jeep before tucking
her car behind a couple of trucks and going inside. A

dozen people were scattered at the various tables; she chose a table in the far corner and smiled at the waitress with the spaniel eyes. Infinitesimally the drooping corners of the waitress's mouth produced what might be called a smile. Much encouraged, Laura ordered spaghetti and a salad and took out her book.

The spaghetti was excellent, for Annie had not skimped on the spices and the garlic, and Laura was served the same warm, yeasty rolls as before. She ate two, knowing she would have to go for a run tomorrow to work them off. The book she had brought was a vintage Dick Francis. She was deep into the perils of being an honest bloodstock agent, her fork entwined with long strands of spaghetti, when someone pulled out a chair at her table and sat down. She raised her eyes, dropped her fork, and said loudly, 'Go away.'

Tight-lipped, Charles said, 'I've been looking for you for the past three hours. Or had you forgotten we were supposed to eat together?'

'I don't eat with people who lose their tempers and treat me like dirt and accuse me of eavesdropping when I turn up unexpectedly at their door,' she said in one breath. 'I was enjoying my dinner until you came along. Will you please leave?'

'I have just as much right to be in this restaurant as you do. And I came to apologise.'

'If you don't go away, I shall embarrass both of us by picking up my dinner and moving to another table.'

Charles leaned his long-limbed body back in the chair. 'You can't embarrass me that easily, Laura. Anyway, I shall only follow you. From table to table if necessary. Who'll give up first, do you think?'

She grabbed for her handbag. 'In that case I shall pay for my dinner and leave altogether.'

'It certainly causes less fuss when you pay, doesn't it?' His hand clamped around her wrist. 'Leave your handbag where it is. Because you're not going anywhere until I've had a chance——'

Archie staggered up to their table, pulled out a third chair and said blearily, 'Evenin', all.'

He reeked of rum. Laura reached over with her free hand, detached Charles's fingers from her wrist, picked up her fork and took a healthy mouthful of spaghetti. Let Charles deal with Archie.

Charles tried. 'Archie, I shall be glad to talk to you later. I'll even drive you home, which by the look of you is something of a necessity. But right now I'm in the middle of a private conversation with this lady——'

'He means we're in the middle of a fight, Archie,' Laura said sweetly. 'You may stay as long as you like. In fact, I'll buy you a coffee.'

With ominous calm Charles said, 'Laura, you're only delaying the inevitable. Sooner or later you're going to hear me out. If I have to bloody well kidnap you.'

She gave him a poisonous look. 'Oh, I'm sure you're quite capable of it.'

The waitress shuffled up to the table. 'Dessert, ma'am?'

'Please,' said Laura. 'What is there?'

'Apple and cherry pie, lemon meringue pie and bread pudding. Ice cream extra.'

'Lemon meringue pie and coffee, please. And a coffee for this gentleman.' She indicated Archie and added, 'The other man is leaving.'

'Wrong, Laura,' Charles said evenly. 'I'll have a coffee too, please. Along with apple pie and ice cream.'

'You can take it to a different table,' Laura snapped.

The waitress looked understandably confused, her stub of a pencil hovering over her order pad. Charles repeated patiently, 'That's three coffees, one lemon pie and one apple pie with ice cream. All to this table.'

Patently relieved, the waitress copied everything down and disappeared. Charles looked Laura in the eye and added, 'The apology, having waited for three hours, will survive a further delay, I'm sure.'

'I do not wish to discuss it,' Laura said grandly.

'You're damn well going to whether you want to or not.'

'You two fighting again?' said a contralto voice rich with amusement. 'Chuck, she's a nice girl—you shouldn't pick on her so much.'

Charles raked his fingers through his hair. 'I'm trying to apologise to her, Annie!'

'Didn't look much like an apology to me,' said Annie comfortably. 'How was the spaghetti, dear?'

'Wonderful!' Laura said. 'I've even got my wallet tonight, so I can pay for it.'

'That's good. Chuck, you gotta learn to look like you're sorry when you apologise. Not like you're gonna cut her throat.'

'It's a toss-up which I'll do first,' Charles said caustically. 'And don't call me Chuck.'

Annie gave him a considering look, then diverted her attention to Archie. 'Archie, you go back to your table now. These two got some patching up to do.' As the waitress approached, Annie deftly put the desserts and two of the cups of coffee on the table and waved the last cup of coffee and Archie to a corner table. 'Over there. But you'll give him a drive home, won't you, Chuck?'

'Yes, I'll give him a drive home.'

Archie pushed himself upright, pronounced to the world in general, 'The path of true love rarely runs smooth,' and obediently followed the waitress and his coffee to the table in the corner.

'Isn't that the truth?' Annie remarked rhetorically, and winked at Laura. 'Enjoy your pie, dear.' With an air of having done her best for them, she trundled back to the kitchen.

Charles glared at his apple pie as if not quite sure how it got there. 'I wonder if there's the slightest chance that we can get this whole scene from the level of farce to some degree of realism.'

Laura took a mouthful of pie. The meringue was a crisp, golden brown and the filling tangy with lemon. 'I

would doubt it,' she said, as in the corner Archie started
to sing a rather dubious sea shanty. 'Is your pie as good
as mine?'

'Laura, for God's sake . . .'

She glanced up, for there was genuine pleading in his
voice rather than anger. She said with complete
honesty, 'Charles, I wasn't deliberately listening to your
conversation. I happened to drop in then, that's all.'
She poked at the meringue with her fork. 'The way you
acted really upset me. There was no reason for you to
be as angry as you were.'

He shoved his plate to one side and took her hands in
his. 'Do you think I don't know that? Laura, I'm sorry
for the way I behaved—it was unpardonable.

In a small voice she said, 'Then why did you do it?'

His fingers tighted their hold. 'Look at me,' he said.
'There's a reason why I behaved the way I did. A very
good reason. But I can't tell you what it is. Not yet.
Someday soon I hope I can. But until then I have to ask
you to trust me—and to forgive me for what must
appear to you as an unwarranted attack.'

'Are you doing something illegal?' she whispered.

The look of stunned disbelief of his face could not
possibly have been an act. 'Illegal?' he repeated blankly.

'I couldn't understand why else you would be so
upset that I'd overheard you.'

'No, Laura. Nothing illegal, nothing morally wrong.
I can assure you of that.'

She believed him; which left unsolved the mystery of
why he had behaved as he had. 'It was as if you'd
changed into a different person,' she said. 'One I hadn't
seen before.'

'Before you go home at the end of the month I hope
to be able to explain to you everything you don't
understand. I know that must sound like a cop-out, but
I don't know how else to handle this. There *is* a reason
for my behaviour, it's desperately important to me, and
very personal.' He began to pour sugar into his coffee,
his attention only partially on what he was doing.

'There's nothing else I can say . . . except to ask you to forgive me.'

'You take a lot of sugar,' she remarked irrelevantly.

His smile was derisory. 'To sweeten me up.'

She began to eat the lemon meringue pie again, her eyes downcast. Trust me, he was saying. Forgive me. Formidable words, trust and forgiveness, emotions not easily or lightly bestowed.

As if he had read her thoughts, Charles said bitterly, 'I'm asking a hell of a lot, aren't I? I won't blame you if you're still angry with me, Laura.'

'I'm not angry,' she said. 'Confused, maybe. But not angry.'

'Thank God for that,' he said fervently. Half-standing, he leaned over the table and kissed her, and in the corner Archie began to clap.

Not knowing what else to do, Laura picked up her fork, ate the last piece of pie and drained her coffee cup. 'I got quite a bit of studying done today,' she said finally, guessing they both needed a neutral subject to discuss.

'Good for you . . . by the way, why did you drop by this afternoon—for a coffee break, or did you have a specific reason?'

She remembered the sharp-edged tracks in the sand and smiled at him, her face softening as she described that mystical sense of another presence with whom she had shared the stretch of beach and the meadow. 'I never did see the deer,' she finished slowly. 'But maybe I didn't need to.'

'And that was why you came, to tell me about the deer?'

'Mmm . . . I wanted to share it with someone.'

'And you got your head bitten off instead,' he said ruefully. 'Look, I'm going to take Archie home. Can I drop in for a few minutes afterwards?'

Drop in was a euphemism, she knew. If he came, he would stay longer than a few minutes; if he stayed, he would almost undoubtedly kiss her; if he kissed her, they could well end up in bed together. She did not want to make love to him tonight, not with the memory of his anger still so fresh in her mind. 'I'd rather you didn't,' she said. 'I'm very tired.'

'Have I scared you off, Laura?' His mouth had an unhappy twist. 'That was not my intention.'

'Perhaps you have,' she said honestly. 'I've had enough confusion for one day, I do know that.'

He bit his lip in frustration. 'Tomorrow I've got some work to do that I can't put off any longer, and then in the evening I'm tied up with the basketball team. But the day after is free. Why don't we take off, Laura—go up to the northern part of the island, go to the beach, maybe have dinner in the Highlands Park. Would you like to do that?'

Her smile was troubled. 'Yes, I would. But——'

'Good. I'll pick you up early. Bring a dress for dinner, hmm? And now I'd better take Archie home.' He pushed back his chair.

Annie must have been watching. She sailed through the swing doors just as they approached the cash register, rang up their bills and said in the nearest thing to a conspiratorial whisper that she could manage, 'Are you two still mad at each other? Or did you make up?'

'No, we're not and yes, we did,' said Charles. 'Mind your own business, Annie my love.'

'You're one of my best customers, Chuck. So you are my business.' Annie laughed loudly at her own joke and passed Laura her change. 'There you are, dear. Don't do anything I wouldn't do, would you?' A coy wink. 'Which gives you lots of leeway.'

Annie being coy was more than Laura could cope with. She muttered something incoherent and headed for the door, her cheeks pink. Charles and Archie followed in her wake. Outside she hurried towards her car as if she had any number of important things to do, calling over her shoulder, 'See you the day after tomorrow, Charles. Good night, Archie.' She was running away, or postponing the inevitable. She wasn't sure which.

CHAPTER SIX

LAURA had planned to spend the next day cold-bloodedly analysing her relationship with Charles, placing him in perspective, sorting out and thereby dissipating the emotions he aroused. An impossible task, as she soon discovered, for he defied analysis and refused to be categorised, and her emotions remained in a lamentable state of confusion. Giving up, she immersed herself in the chapters on alkenes and alkynes, finding in the precision and orderliness of chemistry an antidote to her own lacerated feelings. She called home, discovering that Sue-Ann, Keith and Darren were doing very well without her. She walked on the beach, watching the clouds scud across the sky and the whitecaps dance on the water. She thought about Charles, his anger and his laughter, his lean body and hungry kisses, and of how she was drawn to him like the brown-winged moths to the light over Annie's door. But light can burn; and moths dance themselves to exhaustion . . .

Almost she hoped she would wake the next morning to a storm, rain and wind that would cancel the outing with Charles. But on the contrary she woke to sunlight and singing birds, and when she peered through the bedroom curtains saw an immaculate July morning. It's fate, she thought. You can't fight fate. And abandoned herself to the anticipation of a whole day spent with Charles, an anticipation that was to be fully justified.

Because the bruises on her shins were a mosaic of yellow, purple and pink, she wore trousers, very tight white trousers with a shocking pink shirt that tied beneath her breasts. Charles gave a loud and, for Laura, very satisfying whistle when he came to the door to get her. She said primly, 'If I wore shorts, you might get arrested for having assaulted me.'

He eyed her trousers. 'This way you might get arrested for indecent exposure.'

'They're not *that* tight.'

'Tight enough to do damage to my blood pressure.' He smiled at her. 'Hello, Laura. If I kiss you good morning we may never leave—we may head straight to the bedroom.'

He kissed her anyway, a kiss that sent her heart rate soaring. Epinephrine increases heart rate and cardiac output, she thought confusedly. Epinephrine is a secretion of the adrenal medulla.

In an excess of high spirits Charles picked her up and swung her round in a circle. 'It's a beautiful day, we're going to the most beautiful part of Cape Breton and I'm in the company of a beautiful woman—what more could I ask?'

Laura forgot about the adrenal medulla, for his *joie de vivre* was contagious and set the tone for the day, which she was long to remember as one of the happiest of her life. They bypassed Sydney and crossed Bras d'Or on the huge metal span of Seal Island Bridge, below which the tides churned past the lighthouse; on the other side of Kelly's Mountain they took the little cable ferry across St Ann's Bay. Terns screamed overhead. The tree-clad mountains tumbled vertically to the sea. The road stretched out before them, beckoning them northward. An hour's drive along the rocky coastline brought them to the Highlands National Park, which stretched from coast to coast across an interior of bogs, scrub spruce and trout-filled lakes. Moose, lynx and foxes roamed the hills; the sky above was home for eagles and ospreys.

Charles had brought a picnic lunch. They ate perched on the rocks at the foot of Mary Ann Falls, spray drifting to cool their skin, the roil of the peat-brown waters and the rattle of stones casting a hypnotic spell on them. Dragonflies, iridescent in the sunlight, darted among the fern fronds that curved gracefully over the pool. The water was ice-cold.

Two families that included several very noisy children clambered down the path to the base of the falls. One of the children threw a pop can in the water, shieking with glee as it bobbed on the waves. Charles raised an expressive eyebrow at Laura and packed up the remnants of their food, being very careful to leave no trace of their presence. 'Shall we go?'

'By all means. I swear no child of mine will ever do a thing like that!'

He smiled at her indignation. 'I'm sure it won't . . . shall we head for the beach?'

They spent the afternoon lazing in the sun, swimming, and playing with a beach ball. Salt and sand soon encrusted Laura's skin. She ran from the chill of the sea to the heat of the beach as carefree as a child, yet, because of Charles, achingly conscious of being a woman. She lay beside him on the sand; she rubbed suntan lotion on his back; she ran hand in hand with him into the waves; and inwardly she longed for everyone else on the beach to vanish, leaving her and Charles alone to make love to each other, slow, sensuous love, their bodies drugged by the sweetness of summer.

Charles had friends who owned a condominium at the foot of the ski slope, and had already arranged that he and Laura go there to shower and change for dinner. His friends, Peter and Danielle, were pleasant, relaxed and hospitable, making Laura feel instantly at home. A hot shower felt heavenly. She dried her hair, took considerable care with her make-up, and put on a flowered, very feminine sundress with delicate high-heeled sandals and a lacy white shawl; in the mirror she saw the shine of happiness in her brown eyes, smiled at herself and went back to the living room.

Charles was using the downstairs bathroom. Laura accepted a glass of champagne, and in answer to Peter's tactful probing described her life in the Annapolis

Valley and her ambitions to be a doctor. Innocently, into a gap in the conversation, she said, 'Have you known Charles long?'

'Seventeen or eighteen years,' Peter replied. 'We went to school together and then to university. When Charles went to work for his father, we rather lost touch. Then, of course, he spent the last couple of years gallivanting around the world. So we haven't seen much of him lately. I was delighted when he 'phoned a couple of months ago and told us he was in the area for the summer.'

It was the first Laura had heard of Charles travelling around the world. How little she knew of him ... yet she could not very well ask Peter about Charles's parents and upbringing and job. Peter would assume she knew all those things. But Peter would be wrong. She took a heady gulp of champagne and decided it was time she was given a few answers.

Charles in a lightweight, beautifully tailored suit rather took her breath away. Charles of the Ritz, she thought faintly, remembering her initial impression that, chameleon-like, he would fit into any environment. What was his background that he could drink coffee with Archie in Annie's restaurant and champagne with Peter and Danielle in a living room that unobtrusively spoke of money and good taste, and look equally at home in both?

They ate dinner at Keltic Lodge, a resort hotel built on a narrow peninsula so that the dining room overlooked the ocean on either side. Laura sipped her gin and tonic and said casually, 'Charles, we've never really talked about you—your parents, your family, your background. I realised when I was talking to Peter how little I actually know about you.'

He poured Coke over the rum and ice in his glass. 'Not really much to tell,' he said, as casually as she. 'My father's a businessman, president of his own mining company. Ambitious, compulsive, likes power. Always wanted me in the business. I took a master's degree in

business administration—as did Peter—worked for my
father for three years, couldn't hack it, freelanced for a
while, then took off round the world. Gesture of
independence, you could call it. My father and I are
now in the process of working out a new relationship,
which is more difficult for him than for me. I'll head
back up that way in the autumn.'

'Do you have any brothers and sisters?'

'No. Only child—makes the pressures worse, of
course.'

'Your mother?'

'Mother does as Father says, and thinks I should do
likewise.'

His voice was clipped, giving nothing away. 'Were
you happy as a child?' she persisted.

'Happy enough, I suppose. Left to my own devices a
lot.'

'What was your house like?' A six-room bungalow or
a thirty-room mansion? But she did not quite have the
gall to be so openly curious.

'Oh, average.' Restlessly he shifted in his chair in a
way she had come to recognise. 'You know, I could say
the same of you. You've told me quite a bit about your
niece and nephews, but not about your parents and
childhood.'

'I did have a happy childhood, no question of it. And
in a sense I was like an only child, because James was
nineteen years older than me and my parents had no
other children. My father used to call me the
afterthought.' She smiled reminiscently. 'My father
owned his own business, too—although on a much
more modest scale than yours, I'm sure. He was a
mechanic and owned a garage. He was a good
mechanic, too, a perfectionist with a feel for cars. So he
had customers who'd been with him for years ... I
leanred a lot from my father. To do the best you can at
whatever you do. To deal honestly with people. And in
a strange way my ambition to be a doctor stemmed
from him. He loved figuring out what was wrong with

an engine and making it work better, and I suppose I transferred that to people.'

'Does he still own the garage?'

'Yes. Although he may retire soon, he's in his sixties.'

'And your mother?'

'Very strict but also very fair, and with the saving grace of a sense of humour. I relate better to my father, no question of that.'

'Where do they live?'

'Toronto.' Had she been watching Charles's face, she would have seen wariness flicker across it; but she was squeezing the slice of lime against the side of her glass. 'I lived at home while I did my undergraduate degree— one reason for my somewhat constricted social life. My parents have old-fashioned standards, and I figured while I was living under their roof I should abide by those standards.' She gave a philosophical shrug. 'Just as well, actually. I'm sure I studied harder because I lived at home.'

'But you said you had an affair during those years.'

So he had remembered. 'I fell madly in love with a pre-law student who had his own apartment. Maybe one of the reasons it didn't work very well for me was because I felt I was deceiving my parents. The old guilt-trip. They would have been horrified, I know.'

The waitress brought fish chowder in two-handled cups. As she moved away Charles said quietly, 'Would you feel guilty if you were to have an affair with me?'

Laura gulped a mouthful of soup, gasping as it burned its way down her throat. 'You do choose your moments!'

'Sorry.' Although he did not look sorry. 'Would you, Laura?'

'Is that a rhetorical question?'

'By no means. You're a chemistry graduate—you know as well as I do what happens when we come within ten feet of each other. An affair is a logical extension of that.'

'Logical?'

'Not a very good word, I agree. Nothing logical about the way I feel about you.'

'How do you feel about me?' she said in a low voice.

'As though I will not rest until I have you in my bed.'

'Oh.' She dropped her eyes.

'On a more platonic level I really like you. I feel as though we're becoming friends.' She was silent, for the simple reason that she did not know what to say. 'Believe me, Laura, I know about the guilt parents can load on their children. If an affair would do you more harm than good,' he gave her a smile that touched her heart, 'then I'll just have to control my baser instincts when I'm around you.'

He deserved an answering honesty. 'I need more time,' she said, then recognised to her horror an echo of what she had said to Bart. 'I don't know you well enough, I've only just met you,' she stumbled on. 'I know the chemistry's there, I'd have to be a fool not to, but that's never happened to me before, and I—I can't . . .'

'It's never happened to me, either.'

'Your fiancée?'

'Economics was the discipline operating in that relationship, not chemistry. And I can counter by saying what about your fiancé?'

'He never really was a fiancé.' She added succinctly, knowing her words for the truth, 'Loneliness—not chemistry.'

Charles said gently, 'Let's cool it for a while then, Laura. No more passionate embraces, no more kisses that go on forever.' He extended his hand across the table. 'A deal?'

She shook hands, feeling the familiar current of awareness course from his hand to hers in a way that made nonsense of their pact. 'A deal,' she said solemnly.

'The soup's getting cold.'

She addressed herself to the chowder. Charles liked her, wanted her for a friend, wanted to have an affair with her; why then did she have the feeling that the real issues had not been dealt with? Had not even been defined? 'I don't even know how old you are,' she complained.

'Almost thirty-one.'

'When's your birthday? Really, Charles, information has to be dragged out of you!'

'A week from next Wednesday.'

'Truly? You must come for dinner at my place that day,' she said spontaneously.

He hesitated. 'Why don't I take you out for dinner instead?'

'Goodness, no. I treat you on your birthday. You take me out on my birthday. At home I always throw a party for Keith and for Sue-Ann. Darren isn't as sociable, so I cook a special dinner of all his favourites for him. What are your favourites?'

There was a strange note in Charles's voice. 'I like fish. Of any kind.'

'Then that's what you shall have.'

'Did your parents always treat birthdays as occasions?'

'Indeed they did.' Her face clouded. 'I haven't seen as much of them as I would like the last four years. There just wasn't the money to go back and forth. Or the time.'

'Has money, or rather the lack of it, been a problem, Laura?'

'It has rather, yes. James had a history of heart trouble, you see, so his insurance was barely adequate. Luckily he owned the house outright and made some wise investments, or else we'd really have been in trouble.' This, she knew, was part of the reason she had been unable to go on a wild spending spree when she had won the lottery. She couldn't break the habits of years.

'But Sue-Ann's nearly ready for university, Keith wants to study music and you want to go to medical school—how will you manage?'

A million dollars should cover it. 'Haven't you heard of student loans?' Laura said with a brittle smile, hating herself for lying to him yet knowing she was not ready to share with him the story of her wealth. She wanted to be loved for herself, not for her money. So did that mean she wanted Charles to fall in love with her?

He hadn't yet, that was certain. Liking, friendship and lust did not add up to love. And what of herself? What did she feel for him? A strong physical attraction, she told herself. That's all. She smiled at the waitress as she removed their plates and began to discuss the pros and cons of specialisation after a general medical degree.

The conversation did not return to matters of love or lust. After they had talked about books they had read and films they had seen, Charles described some of his travels in the Far East. They laughed a lot; and when they went outside Charles scrupulously kept his distance as they wandered back to the car in the moonlight, the air heavy with the scent of roses, the sea awash with silvery light: a setting the epitome of romance, and all wasted.

Laura slept some of the way home. Charles deposited her at the door of her cottage, said sincerely, 'Thanks, Laura, I had a wonderful day. See you tomorrow,' and left. She let herself in, and very conscious of a sense of deflation went to bed.

Laura woke up the next morning determined to think about money. After clearing away the breakfast dishes, she got out a big sheet of paper and a pencil with an eraser and sat down at the table by the window. At the top of the paper she wrote $1,000,000. She radiated a series of lines out from it. Then she sat and stared at the paper for a very long time.

She was not going to marry Bart. That decision had somehow looked after itself in the few days she had been here; meeting Charles had had a fair bit to do with it. Therefore she would presumably be studying medicine not in Halifax but in Toronto. (Toronto is where Charles is from.) She knew she could not live with her parents again, fond of them as she was; after managing her own life for the past four years, she would not be able to cope with the role of an obedient daughter. A sensible course of action would be to buy her own house near the university and live in it. Real estate, so she had been told, was always a sound investment. At the bottom of one of the lines she wrote: buy house or condominium in Toronto. Hesitating, she added $150,000, followed by a large question mark.

The cost of medical school took up another line, education for Sue-Ann and Keith another. She added an equivalent sum of money for Darren; if he wanted to buy a car with it, he could. Then she spent several more minutes doodling aimlessly on the paper. She should invest in a pension fund. And no doubt she should paint the steeple. She drew a picture of a church with a steeple, embellishing it with a rose window and a bell.

Brightening, she wrote at the bottom of another line, trip for Mum and Dad. Her mother had always wanted to go south in the winter.

Deciding, not for the first time, that a large amount of money carried with it a fair degree of social responsibility, Laura got up to make a cup of coffee. Yesterday's sunshine had been usurped by a steady rain. A good day to study. Also a good day to make chocolate chip cookies, she thought. She'd study much more effectively with something to nibble on. So the air was redolent with the scent of chocolate and freshly baked dough when Charles knocked on the door and called, 'May I come in?' Joining her in the kitchen, he eyed the heaped-up rack of cookies and said, 'Those look good.'

She laughed. 'You followed your nose all the way from your place. Help yourself.'

He bit into one. 'You could be useful to have around.'

'None of that male chauvinistic talk—a woman's place is not necessarily the kitchen.'

'You mean it's the bedroom?' he asked innocently.

'For that you can make your own coffee.'

He put on the kettle. 'I have to go into town and wondered if you needed anything.'

'If you'd get me some milk, it would save me a trip to the store. It's a lousy day, isn't it?'

He wandered over to the window. 'Settled in for the day. Good thing we went north yesterday.'

Laura took a mug out of the cupboard, added instant coffee and three teaspoons of sugar, and heard him say, amusement in his voice. 'You must have bought a lottery ticket, did you? Funny, I'd have thought you were too practical to imagine how you'd spend money you haven't won yet.'

She almost dropped the mug. Peering round the corner she saw Charles looking at the sheet of paper with $1,000,000 written at the top. Oh no ... she swallowed hard and said, 'Goes to show you don't know me very well yet. Don't we all dream about what we'd do with a million dollars?'

'You strike me as a doer, not a dreamer. I didn't peek, Laura—what would you do with a million?'

'Pay for medical school, buy a house and send my parents on a world cruise.'

'You could invest the money and not bother with medical school at all.'

'You *do* know me better than that, Charles.'

'So I do. May I have another cookie—or two?'

'You're as bad as Keith. Help yourself.' She took the last baking tray out of the oven. 'I love baking on a rainy day. I make a lot of bread in the winter.' And the subject of the million dollars was, to her great relief, dropped. As soon as he had gone—without kissing her—she folded the paper up, shoved it in a drawer and got out her organic chemistry text.

Two hours later Laura took a break for a late lunch, then went back to the book again. She was pleased with her progress, for she was discovering she had not forgotten as much as she would have thought after a gap of four years. The medical admissions tests covered biology, physics, chemistry, mathematics and English; she was determined to do well in all the subjects, although she knew she would leave reviewing the physics, her *bête noir,* until the last.

At five-thirty she heard the crunch of tyres in the gravel. Charles, with the milk. He stepped inside. 'Have you been studying all day?'

'Mmm . . . I got a lot done.'

'Time to quit. Do you like walking in the rain?'

She smiled. 'Well, yes. But——'

'Good. Get your raincoat and boots on.'

She tilted her head to one side. '. . . please, Laura?'

He took her by the shoulders, said levelly, 'When you look at me like that all my good intentions go out of the window,' and kissed her firmly and without hurry.

How can the world stop just because a man kisses you? Laura said faintly, 'We're going for a walk.'

'Outside.'

'In the rain.'

'The cold-shower principle.'

He had, finally, stepped back from her. 'I'll get my rain gear,' she said, and fled into her room where he could not see how her hands were shaking.

Attired in yellow sou'westers and rainwear, the two of them set off down the shore. Instead of deer tracks in the sand there were the tiny indentations of a million raindrops. Sky and sea were grey, the line between them blurred.

They walked fast, Laura enjoying the coolness of the rain against her face as they chatted inconsequentially about this and that. Taking a deep breath of the damp air, she said suddenly, 'This was a great idea—I was feeling cooped up without really knowing it.'

He looked down at her. Her skin and the tendrils of hair on her forehead were wet; her face was innocent of make-up; her smile was friendly, happy, without guile. He said, 'Laura, you don't know how glad I am to know you. You're so different from anyone I've ever met before.'

She stood still. The rain dripped from her sou'wester on to her jacket. 'I am?' she said blankly.

'You're honest and direct. You're ambitious and brave. And you've certainly got a strong sense of responsibility.'

'You make me sound like some kind of a saint.'

A smile softened the seriousness of his expression. 'I should add quick-tempered and stubborn . . . also, of course, heart-stoppingly beautiful.'

'Charles,' she protested. 'I'm only ordinary. Truly. My father's a mechanic, my brother was a small-town bank manager. I——'

'That's got nothing to do with it, as well you know . . . I say I'm glad I've met you, and so I am. But I have this sense of time rushing by. You've been here a week already. The month will be gone before we know it.'

She could feel the heavy thud of her heart, which had nothing to do with the speed at which they had been walking. Trying to joke, she said, 'That's my vacation you're dispensing with so cavalierly.'

He gripped her by the shoulders hard enough that through her layers of clothing she could feel the separate imprints of his fingers. 'I'm serious, Laura. I'll be staying until the end of the summer. Can't you stay longer?'

'No. Of course not. I shouldn't really be away this long as it is.'

'Then can I come and visit you in August?'

She tried to pull away. 'It's a long way, a six-or seven-hour drive.'

'I could fly to Halifax and you could meet me there.'

Relief flooded her face. 'That would be a much better idea, I love the city!'

He did not smile back. 'Are you saying you don't want to take me to your home?'

She gaped at him. That was exactly what she was saying; because if he went to Grantham, he would find out she was a rich woman and everything would be changed. He, like Bart, might then propose . . . and it would break her heart if he did. 'N-no,' she stammered. 'But you don't know what it's like having a bunch of teenagers underfoot. Loud music. No privacy. Meals at all kinds of odd hours——'

'Sounds all right to me.' In deliberate challenge he went on, 'I'd like to meet the three of them, Laura.'

'They could meet us in Halifax.'

He gave her a little shake. 'A few moments ago I said you were honest. You're not being honest with me now. What are you hiding, Laura? Why don't you want me to go to the town where you live—whose name, as I'm sure you realise, you've never told me.'

Impaled on the steel-grey eyes, she cried, 'Charles, I'm getting very wet and I do dislike this conversation—can we at least keep moving?'

'We're not going anywhere until you've answered my question. What haven't you told me about your family? Do you live with this lawyer friend of yours? Is that what you don't want me to know?'

'Live with *Bart*? For goodness sake, you don't know small towns very well. Or his mother.'

'Then what is it?' He gave her another shake. 'Is there something wrong with me that you don't want me in your home?'

Beleaguered, she retorted, 'Of course not! Don't be silly.'

'Have you got a crazy old aunt locked up in the attic? Skeletons falling out of every closet? Come clean, Laura—because we're going to stand here in the rain until you do.'

'Oh we are, are we?' Deliberately she relaxed her body in his hold. 'Then you'd better be prepared to get very wet.'

Between gritted teeth he said, 'Has no one ever been tempted to wring your neck?'

'I have no idea. Charles, I am not going to stand here in the rain forever!'

His smile was thoroughly unpleasant. 'I believe we've already established that I'm bigger than you—you may not have any choice.'

'You can make me angrier than anyone I've ever known before,' she said, somewhat redundantly in view of her glittering eyes and flushed cheeks.

'Good. At least you're not indifferent to me.'

'Oh, I've never been that.'

'Yet another thing we have in common ... Laura, if you were genuinely indifferent to me, would you tell me the name of your home town?'

She gave a sigh of defeat. 'Yes, I probably would. Listen to me, Charles. The other day when I overheard your telephone conversation you said you couldn't explain why you were so angry with me. You asked me to trust you. Well, I'm going to do the same thing. I would be happy to meet you in Halifax in August. For the rest, I'm asking you to trust me. I'm not hiding anything I'm ashamed of. I'm not in trouble with the law, I've done nothing wrong—I assure you of that. And that's all I can say.'

'Very clever,' Charles said grimly. 'I can't very well argue, can I? Neatly done, Laura.'

'I'm not trying to be clever!' she burst. 'I'm asking you to extend to me the same trust I've extended to you. Is that so difficult?'

He let go of her shoulders, kicking moodily at the sand with his rubber boots. She added, laughter warming her voice, 'You look like a little boy who's just had his favourite toy taken from him ... You must have dated lots of women—you're not exactly unattractive, you know—and I know you had a fiancée. I can't believe a woman's never made the kind of demand on you that I'm making now. I'm asking you to trust me, that's all.'

He turned to face her. 'Women have made a lot of demands on me, and I include my fiancée among them. But never quite what you're asking. I said you were different, as so you are.'

Thoroughly confused, Laura gazed at him in silence. She said finally, 'Rain is trickling down my neck and my feet are cold. We'd better go back.'

'But nothing's resolved.'

She quoted his own words back to him. 'Don't push the river, it'll flow by itself.'

Intense frustration bit into his features. 'I always thought of myself as a patient man. It took you to show me I was wrong. As wrong as I could be.'

He turned away. Side by side, not touching, they tramped along the beach and through the saturated grass. Then they spoke simultaneously.

'Charles——'

'Laura——'

'You first,' she said.

'Why don't you come over to my place? I'll light the fire and we can cook up something for supper.'

Thank God ... 'Love to,' Laura said.

'What were you going to say?'

'I don't need to say it any more.'

He stopped beside a spruce tree. 'Come on, Laura—say it.'

'I was going to ask if you felt all right about the way we'd left things. But since you've invited me for dinner, I guess you do.'

'I don't. Not really. But I haven't got much choice, have I?' And then he pulled her to him, wet slicker and all, and kissed her. Their sou'westers got entangled and Laura got more water down her neck; but it didn't seem to matter, for his kiss had burned out the anger between them, leaving only a desperate, elemental honesty. She gave him a shaky but radiant smile and grabbed him by the hand. 'Let's run—I'm freezing!'

They were laughing and breathless when they reached the clearing by the cottage. Because the path was narrow Laura had gone ahead; she stopped so suddenly that Charles cannoned into her. His arms went around her. 'What——' he began, and then he saw what she had seen.

A car was parked beside Laura's, a discreetly expensive black sedan. The driver was getting out of his seat to stand by the car, unfurling a black umbrella as he did so. He was wearing tailored grey slacks and a cashmere sweater over an open-necked shirt, and looked as discreetly expensive as his car. He also looked very angry.

'*Bart*!' said Laura.

CHAPTER SEVEN

WITHOUT haste Charles let go of Laura. She straightened
and took a couple of steps towards the black car. 'Bart,
what on earth are you doing here?' Then her voice
changed and the colour drained from her face. 'Is
something wrong? Sue-Ann? The boys?'

'They're fine,' Bart said coldly. 'As always they come
first, don't they?'

'You scared me. I couldn't imagine why you were
here unless something had happened.'

'It wouldn't occur to you that as your fiancé I might
want to see you?'

'You're not my fiancé. I told you I was coming up
here to think things out.'

'And is this, er—gentleman assisting you?'

Laura glowered at him. 'Don't be so pompous.
Charles has the cottage next door, we've been for a
walk, and he put his arms around me because if he
hadn't he'd probably have knocked me flat—I was,
understandably, surprised to see you.'

'Can we continue this discussion indoors?' Bart said
irritably.

She was conscious of a strong reluctance to do so.
'Charles had invited me to his place for dinner.'

'I'm sure Charles will understand that I've driven a
very long way to see you.'

Charles said amiably, 'We'll take a rain check, Laura.
No pun intended.'

She shot a glance at him over her shoulder. He
looked very sure of himself, not at all as she would have
looked had his ertswhile fiancée turned up on the
doorstep of his cottage. He's not the slightest bit
jealous, she thought miserably. I'd much rather he was
breathing fire and telling Bart to get lost.

She said mutinously, 'Only until tomorrow.'

'Tomorrow it is.' Charles patted her cheek in a way that could only be described as brotherly, gave the other man an ironic salute and disappeared into the trees. Laura watched him go, feeling very much abandoned.

Bart said flatly, 'When did you meet him?'

'The day I moved in. Let's go inside, I'm soaked.'

She turned away and climbed the steps to the cottage door. But when she held the door open for Bart, he was not behind her. He was taking a small suitcase out of the boot of his car. She pulled her boots off on the mat inside the door and as he followed her in said bluntly, indicating the suitcase, 'What's that for?'

'It's a suitcase,' he said with heavy sarcasm. 'You put clothes inside it.'

'Why are you bringing it in here?'

'Laura, you don't imagine I'm going to drive back to Grantham tonight, do you?'

'Bart, you are not staying here.'

'And where else do you suggest I stay?'

'There are any number of motels between here and Sydney.'

His movements very precise, Bart folded the umbrella and stood it on the mat. He does look like a watered-down version of Tom Selleck, she thought unkindly. Sue-Ann was right.

He said with irritating composure, 'I've driven several hundred miles in the pouring rain to see you. It's surely not necessary for me to drive another twenty-five or thirty just to find a place to stay. There are two bedrooms here, aren't there?'

He was like a steamroller, flattening all her objections in his path. 'It wouldn't matter if there were fifty bedrooms,' she said tightly.

He gave her the smile that two months ago would have set her heart fluttering in her breast; it radiated sincerity, a sincerity that, had she but known it, had served him well with his female clients over the years.

'Darling Laura,' he said, 'I want to marry you. I've missed you terribly the last few days, so much so that I knew I had to come up here.' Another boyish smile. 'Yes, I know, I should have 'phoned or written. But I came on impulse—I couldn't wait another day. Please don't be angry with me.'

'I'm not angry that you came,' she said more or less truthfully, finishing with complete truth, 'I am angry that you assumed you could stay here.'

'Let's talk about it later,' he coaxed. 'Why don't you take off that very wet jacket and rather odd hat so I can give you a kiss.'

Her sou'wester had not deterred Charles from kissing her. She discovered she did not want to be kissed by Bart. Very slowly she took off her jacket, hanging it on one of the hooks by the door, and undid the strap under her chin. With the sou'wester still in her hand she said flatly, 'Bart, there's no easy way to say this. I can't marry you. I know that now.'

Afterwards she wondered if he had been expecting something of the kind, because all he did was take the hat from her fingers, hang it on the hook and say calmly, 'Darling, I do understand. Your whole life has been turned upside down by that money, hasn't it? I can see why you needed to get away. I didn't understand at the time and perhaps I wasn't very sympathetic. I'm sorry about that . . . I do hope, Laura, that you never in any way equated my proposal with the money. While I was away in Montreal on that course, remember, I realised how much you were on my mind and how much I'd come to care for you. I knew I had to ask you to marry me. And then when I got back you'd won the lottery.' His smile had just the right touch of irony. 'One of those coincidences better suited for fiction than real life.'

She was standing very still, her dark eyes unreadable. Was he being sincere? Or simply very clever, anticipating all her objections before she could make them? 'That's not the point,' she said, giving him the benefit of the doubt and therefore trying to couch her words kindly. 'You see, what I've discovered is that I don't love you. I'm sorry—I feel terrible about it, because I genuinely thought I did love you. But I don't. So I can't marry you.'

For a moment the youthful charm disappeared, ousted by an emotion a great deal more ruthless. Then Bart recovered his poise. 'You're wrong, you know, Laura. You've been in love with me for three years.' He ran his fingers through his hair, causing an engaging disarray of his dark curls. 'Look, I could do with a drink or a cup of coffee. Why don't we continue this later on?'

At least he had not tried to kiss her. She blurted, 'I think I was in love with you because I was lonely and missing Toronto and there wasn't anyone else. Bart, I'm sorry. I've behaved badly if I led you to expect that I'd marry you.'

'A drink, Laura,' he said inflexibly. 'I brought a bottle of vodka with me. Do you have any tomato juice?'

If she couldn't have gin, vodka was her second choice. 'In the refrigerator. I have some chilli I made a couple of days ago, and I'd be happy to share it with you, Bart. But I want you to 'phone a motel and get a reservation for the night.'

'Lots of time—I'll do it after we eat.'

Laura would have preferred him to do it now but knew that, if pushed, he could become totally intractable. She busied herself with measuring rice and putting together a salad while Bart made the drinks. Wrinkling her nose at her first sip, she said, 'You put in a lot of Tabasco.'

'Too much? Sorry . . . drink up and I'll make you a second.'

Because she was on edge, inwardly counting the minutes until he was gone, Laura drained the glass much more rapidly than she would have normally. Bart talked entertainingly about a couple of cases he had just concluded and the latest bestseller he had read; when he put his mind to it, he could be very good company, as well she knew. She started on the second drink, cutting up into a bowl all the fresh fruit she could find. The knife slipped out of her hand a couple of times. Sectioning the oranges seemed much more complicated than usual. She eyed her second drink, which was already half gone, with suspicion. 'Are these doubles?'

'Really, Laura . . . it was the Tabasco I was heavy with.'

More by luck than judgment, because she was feeling peculiarly light-headed, Laura got the meal on the table, chilli steaming, rice fluffy, salad crisp. Bart had topped up her glass. The chilli was strongly spiced so she finished that one as well. He talked on about a movie he had seen in Halifax and from there to the many advantages of living in the city. Laura listened politely, although it was an effort to concentrate. But when he mentioned a house he had seen for sale in the vicinity of the medical school, she snapped to attention. 'If I have my choice, I'll be attending the University of Toronto,' she said.

'I can manage a move to Halifax, Laura, but not to Toronto. Mother couldn't handle that.'

She repressed the impulse to tell him what he could do with his mother. 'You're missing the point—although I'm quite sure I've said all this before. I can't marry you, Bart. Therefore I shall apply to Toronto's medical school. That's home to me.'

He helped himself to a large bowl of fruit salad. 'Let me be perfectly frank with you, Laura. Am I not good enough for you since you won all that money?' As her jaw dropped, he pressed his advantage. 'You were in love with me for three years. Then you won a million dollars and suddenly you're not in love with me anymore. So the only conclusion I can come to is that a small-town lawyer is no longer enough for you. You're setting your sights higher—heading for the big city and bigger game.'

'That's not——'.

'I work hard at my job and I earn a decent salary. But I can never earn anything like a million dollars. I suppose it's natural that you should want more, but I have to admit it hurts. Changed circumstances shouldn't alter relationships or emotions.'

'Stop!' she cried. 'It's not *like* that! If I truly loved you I wouldn't care if you had five cents or five million. But I don't *love* you, Bart. That's the issue—not the money.'

'The money has changed you, Laura,' he said ponderously.

'I don't want it to change me!' It was a cry from the heart.

'I'm very much afraid that it has.'

He was playing with his moustache: a danger signal. Trying hard to marshal her thoughts—how much vodka had he put in those drinks?—Laura went on the attack. 'Since we're being perfectly frank with each other, let me pose a certain question to you. Suppose I'd already taken that one million and given it all away to charity. Every last cent. Would you be here right now, Bart? Pressing me to marry you? Or would you be back in Grantham minding your own business?'

'I resent the implications of that question.'

'Just answer it,' she retorted.

'You're posing a theoretical situation. That's scarcely——'

It was her turn to interrupt. Leaning back in her chair, she began to laugh. 'Maybe it's not.'

He paled, his eyes bulging. '*Laura*——'

She was giggling helplessly. 'Maybe I've already done it.'

'You wouldn't do such a thing!'

She put every ounce of sincerity she possessed into a deliberate, outright lie. 'I already have.'

He slumped back into his chair, weakly tugging at his moustache, eyes dazed. 'You couldn't have . . .'

'But I did,' she repeated, crossing her fingers

behind her back in a supersitious attempt to erase the untruth.

But Bart was not a lawyer for nothing. With an obvious effort he gathered his wits. 'No, you didn't,' he said icily. 'I know you too well, Laura. You might give away all that money if there was only yourself to consider. But you wouldn't deprive Keith and Sue-Ann and Darren, I know you wouldn't. You were lying, weren't you?'

'Yes, I was lying,' she said steadily. 'But I think I got my answer.'

'What do you mean?' He blustered.

'Essentially you're here because of the money, aren't you? Oh, I'm sure I'm not repulsive to you. But without the money I wouldn't be nearly as attractive.'

As he slammed his fist on the table the bottle of salad dressing rocked on its base and Laura jumped. 'All right,' he said. 'So I'm not immune to money. So a million dollars makes a difference. I'd have to be a fool for it to be otherwise.'

So was she a fool to want to be loved for herself? She pushed the question to the back of her mind. 'Perhaps you are just being realistic and perhaps I am far too idealistic,' she replied. 'But that's the way it is. Bart, for the last time, I cannot marry you. Please accept that. Because it's the truth.'

He got up from the table, went into the kitchen and came back a minute later with a drink in his hand, a drink he proceeded to gulp down very rapidly. 'I'm not prepared to accept it.'

'You have no choice,' she said, every bit as coldly as him. 'We have nothing more to say to each other. I'm going to 'phone for a reservation and then I'd like you to be on your way. I'm sorry you had such a long journey for nothing, but I didn't ask you to make it.'

He had emptied his glass. He got up, went back into the kitchen and returned holding the bottle of vodka and a can of tomato juice. To her alarm Laura saw the bottle was nearly empty. He sloshed what was left into his glass and added some juice. Then he said smugly, 'Oh no, I can't leave now, Laura. I know if I were to be stopped by the police I'd be over my limit on the breathalyser. You wouldn't want to be responsible for putting a man on the highway who's had one drink too many, would you? I might cause an accident.' He took a swig of the vodka. 'I might kill someone. You'd have that on your conscience—you wouldn't like that.'

She glared at the empty bottle, conscious of the throbbing in her temples. 'You did pour me doubles.'

'Triples, more likely. That's why I added the extra Tabasco, so you wouldn't know. Thought it might soften you up.' His smile had lost its charm. 'Well, I was wrong. But you're not getting rid of me tonight.'

She gripped the edge of the table. 'You don't know how close I am to throwing something at you. So what's on your mind—a cosy little rape?'

He looked genuinely injured. 'Really, Laura, I wouldn't do that. But I'm sure the gentleman next door will be aware that I've spent the night.'

So was she. 'Darren has any number of words for people like you,' she said tautly. 'If I hadn't had such a strict mother, I'd be tempted to use them. I'm going to make up the bed in the spare room and wash the dishes and then I'm going to bed—my own. You can leave first thing in the morning.'

Expansively he waved his glass. 'You go right ahead.'

Literally shaking with suppressed rage, Laura cleared the table and retreated to the kitchen, where she washed the dishes with more speed than care. Next she found some extra bedding and made up the spare bed. She was folding the quilt over the foot when Bart came to stand in the doorway. Ignoring a sudden unease, she said, 'There's an extra blanket in the cupboard. Towels on the chair.' She moved purposely towards the door. 'Good night.'

He was leaning negligently against the door frame. His eyes were not quite focused, but otherwise there was no outward sign of the amount of alcohol he had drunk. 'Kiss me good night, Laura. For old times' sake.'

'No, thank you,' she said crisply, holding her ground. 'Will you move, please, so I can get through?'

He moved more quickly than she could have anticipated, seizing her by the shoulder and planting a vodka-flavoured kiss on her lips. Infuriated, she pulled free. He was blinking owlishly, obviously pleased with himself.'

'Good *night*! she spat. Whirling, she headed for her room and slammed the door. There was no key. The only moveable piece of furniture was a spindly legged chair. She wedged it under the handle, wishing the legs were a little more substantial. Then she sat down hard on the bed.

Her head was aching. Her mouth was dry. The chilli and the vodka were mingling uneasily in her stomach. And under all these sensations she was aware of being afraid. Bart had never been one to make sexual demands on her. But he had never been one to drink too much either. Nor had she ever seriously crossed him before; she was very much aware of the isolation of the cottage, of the drumming of the rain on the roof, of the darkness pushing at the windowpanes. When she heard him moving around in the living room, she tensed. His steps approached her door and stopped. She watched in horrified fascination as the door handle turned, then was released.

'Laura, you don't have to lock me out.'

The spindly legged chair looked very frail; one good thump at the door would dislodge it. Why had she never taken a course in self-defence?

'I need to talk to you, Laura. Nothing's settled, we can't leave things the way they are.' The handle turned again, more roughly. 'Laura, are you there?'

'Yes, I'm here. Please go away, Bart. I have nothing to say to you.'

'At least open the door so I see you.'

'I'm going to bed,' she said loudly, 'and I'd advise

you to do the same.' She bounced up and down so that the bedsprings creaked. 'Good night.' Then she switched out the light.

He shuffled his feet outside the door, under which a chink of light shone into her room. Then his steps retreated. Silence fell.

Laura sat on the edge of the bed, scarcely moving a muscle. What was he doing? Falling asleep in the armchair? Or planning his next move? He was not a man who gave up easily, particularly when his male pride was at stake.

The silence stretched from seconds into minutes. In spite of herself she could feel her eyes closing and her back slumping. Her head was swimming: a most uncomfortable feeling. Bart must have gone to sleep. She was probably safe to do likewise ... her chin dropped to her chest.

The doorknob rattled and she jerked upright with a cry of alarm. 'Go *away*!' she exploded. 'I hate you, Bartholomew Manning!'

'You're acting hysterically,' he said with cold precision, his voice sounding horribly close.

'It's easy to be hysterical when the other person weighs fifty pounds more than you do.'

'I'm not going to use force! I simply want to talk to you.'

'Then talk.'

'I prefer to see the person I'm talking to.'

'You're out of luck.' Under the combined effects of an aching head, a queasy stomach and that nagging edge of fear, Laura lost patience. 'Bart, go away! Go to bed, go to Grantham, go to hell—but just *go*!'

The handle turned and the panels creaked, as if he were pushing his shoulder against them. She stayed glued to the bed, hovering between panic and a laughter which could indeed be hysterical if it ever got started. The situation was farcical, the stealthy movements of the door handle thoroughly unnerving.

They stopped. Silence descended again. But it was so

far from a peaceful silence that Laura felt her over-stretched nerves reach screaming point. She'd had enough of this. She wasn't going to sit meekly on the bed and wait for Bart to come bursting in, even if all he did want to do was talk. With infinite care not to make any noise she eased her weight off the bed and stood up. Her socked feet soundless on the pine floor, she tiptoed around the foot of the bed. A board creaked. She stood frozen, her heartbeat deafening. Silence from the other side of the door. She crept over to the window.

All the windows in the cottage had been modernised to sliding glass panels with screens on the outside. Grateful for the light spilling under the door, she pushed the window as far open as it would go and eased the clips free on the screen, letting it drop to the ground outside, the scrape of its fall hopefully drowned by the rain. Then she regarded the gap doubtfully. She'd look very foolish if she got stuck; and how she would hate having to ask Bart for help.

Her jaw set, Laura climbed up on the pine blanket box that stood under the window. She swung one leg over the sill, then the other, clutching the upper frame with her hands. Twisting her body sideways, she eased herself through the gap, at the last minute pushing herself off as hard as she could. The sill scraped her ribs. More bruises, she had time to think before her feet hit the ground and she landed with an indignified bump on her behind.

She scrambled upright, feeling the rain beat on her face and her bare arms; she was only wearing a T-shirt and jeans. Taking a moment to get her bearings, not easy because the vodka and the darkness were combining to confuse her, she located the path that would lead her to Charles's cottage. Infinitely preferable to spend the night with Charles than with Bart.

She stumbled down the path, tripping over the coiled roots of the evergreens. Rocks stabbed the soles of her feet. Branches scraped her arms and caught at her hair, boughs slapped her face, and the rain soaked her through. Blindly she staggered on, feeling her way as much as seeing it. I'll be safe with Charles, she thought, and the words echoed crazily in her brain. Safe with Charles, safe with Charles . . .

When the trees opened into a clearing, she sensed the black bulk of his cottage and almost cried out with disappointment. The cottage was in darkness. Screwing up her eyes, she searched for the Jeep and could not see it. Charles was out. When she needed him, he was out.

It would not have taken much for Laura to sit down on the grass and howl her eyes out. However, she was not Donald Walker's daughter for nothing. Her father was a tenacious man and had bequeathed a fair share of that resource to Laura. Her chin firmed. So Charles was out . . . she would wait inside for him; and if the door was locked, she'd get in through one of the windows. After all, if she could get out of one cottage through the window, she could get into another the same way. She headed for the steps and tripped over the bottom one, banging her already painful shins and making rather a lot of noise. Oh Charles, why did you have to be out?

Having reached the top step, no small accomplishment, Laura grasped the door handle, breathed a quick prayer and turned it. The door opened.

Scarcely believing her luck, she stood immobile in the rain. The door was open. She could go in.

She did so, softly closing it behind her. She'd lock it once she found a light switch. She wasn't going to risk Bart getting in as well.

She stood still for a moment, trying to get her bearings. The inside of the cottage seemed darker than the outdoors, nor could she remember where the furniture was placed. The only sound was the humming of the refrigerator.

If she assumed that Charles's cottage was wired the same way as hers, the nearest switch should be on the wall to the left. Cautiously Laura began to move in that direction.

She did not even see her attacker. From behind her

an arm strong as steel clamped her body. A leg was hooked around her feet. A hand covered her mouth, smothering her instinctive cry of terror. She wriggled frantically—and ineffectually—and the self-defence course that she had never taken once again flashed across her brain.

Fractionally the arm loosed its hold. She squirmed, the softness of her breast touched the rigid arm, and a male voice said, 'What the hell . . . *Laura*?'

She sputtered something under the hand that still covered her mouth. The hand was removed. A light was switched on, and she blinked up into Charles's face.

He looked appalled. And so he should, she thought dizzily, adding sore ribs to her list of injured parts. Swaying a little on her feet, she said with great dignity, 'I am not trying to steal the family silver.'

Two frown lines appeared on his forehead. He bent his head and sniffed her breath. 'You're drunk,' he said.

Her heart was still shivering in her breast; the rest of her was shivering with cold. 'I am not,' she protested. 'I only had three——' Her eyes widened. What little colour was left in her face vanished. Cupping a hand over her mouth, she pivoted and fled to the bathroom. She had the presence of mind to slam the door behind her.

Five minutes later, having lost vodka, chilli and salad, Laura was standing by the sink splashing cold water on her face. She found some mouthwash in the medicine cabinet and gargled with great thoroughness. She had been aware of Charles standing outside the door saying periodically, 'Laura, are you all right?' and was finally able to say, 'I'm okay. I'll be right out.' Grimacing at the pale face in the mirror, she opened the door.

He surveyed her from head to foot, an expression on his face that she had trouble deciphering, such a mixture it was of concern, laughter, suspicion, and indisputably, tenderness. She said feebly, 'Hello.'

'I'll turn on the bath and lend you some clothes.
Explanations later.'

A ghost of a smile touched her mouth. 'Good idea.'

A hot bath and the donning of pyjamas and a
bathrobe that obviously belonged to Charles did
wonders for Laura's morale. She dried and brushed her
hair and regarded herself in the mirror with rather more
favour. And now for the explanations . . .

Charles had a fire crackling in the hearth, and pillows
and a quilt heaped on the floor in front of it. Laura
huddled into the quilt and rested her back against the
armchair. Briefly she closed her eyes, feeling the heat of
the fire on her skin. 'That feels better,' she breathed
with unmistakable sincerity.

Charles sat down across from her. 'Do you want
anything to eat? Or drink?'

She shuddered. 'No!'

Her eyes were still closed. There were blue smudges
under them, but a little colour had crept into her cheeks
and she was no longer shivering. He said flatly, 'Give.'

Only then did she open her eyes, first gazing into the
dancing, orange-hearted flames, then shifting reluctantly
to him. He was wearing dark cords and a navy
turtleneck sweater, clothes in which he looked solid and
very real. She said, 'This is all going to sound extremely
silly.'

'Give, Laura.'

Fumbling for words, Laura described how Bart had
carried his suitcase into her cottage and the argument
about a motel. She described the Tabasco-laced vodkas
and the chilli, and his insistence that he was going to
marry her. 'Then he proceeded to finish all the vodka.
So he couldn't leave, he wasn't in any state to drive.
Then he—he kissed me. But only once,' she added
hastily. 'I made up the spare bed, went into my own
room and put a chair under the door handle . . . I
know, I've seen too many gangster movies. But I was
frightened, Charles, even though I can't really tell you
why.'

'Try.'

She ticked off the reasons on her fingers. 'He's bigger than me. He'd had too much to drink. He was angry because I wouldn't agree to marry him. ... But that's really all. I don't think he'd have tried to rape me, or anything like that.' Her brow crinkled. 'I don't think Bart's very highly sexed, to tell you the truth. Too fond of his mother, by half.'

'So why did you arrive on my front doorstep in your socked feet in the dead of night and creep inside as if you were a thief?'

'I thought you were out!' she said indignantly. 'I couldn't see the Jeep.'

'I park it in the little shed behind the cottage when it rains, otherwise sticky stuff from the pine trees gets all over it.'

'Well, I didn't know that. Did you really think I was a thief?'

'I certainly did. I'd gone to bed but I couldn't sleep. When I heard you on the steps outside I got up, threw on my clothes, and grabbed you before you could murder me in my bed.'

'Figuratively speaking,' she said gravely.

'Just so. Did I hurt you?'

'Oh, no. I love being squashed and gagged and tripped.'

'Had I known it was you, my approach might have been different.'

She made a face at him. 'Good luck to you. Do you mean that soaking wet, not-very-sober women turn you on?'

'When they're you, yes.'

She said with perfect truth, although with a glint of mischief in her eyes, 'I've got a headache.'

'You're quite safe tonight,' he said cryptically. 'Now answer the question, Laura—why did you leave your cottage?'

She hugged her knees, staring into the flames. 'Well, there I was sitting on my bed in the dark and there was

Bart on the other side of the door wanting to get in. To talk, he said.' She shrugged. 'It could have been the truth. But I could see the handle of the door turning, and then he tried pushing against the panels. And I'd drunk all that vodka and it was raining and pitch dark ... I was scared, Charles. Even though I'm sure Bart would never forget himself and do anything violent, I was scared. It was all so nebulous and yet so—' she sought for the right word, '—so sinister. So I got out through the window and came over here. He said I was acting hysterically, and maybe I was.'

'I don't think you were, Laura. There's the old cliché that it's better to be safe than sorry. Bart was drunk and he was angry. I think you were wise to get out.'

She let out her breath in a tiny sigh. 'I'm glad you think so.' And because she was very tired, she added naïvely, 'I wouldn't want you thinking I behaved hysterically. I'd like you to think well of me.'

He leaned forward, resting a hand on her knee. 'I do, Laura. You must know that.'

Not the words of high-flown romance. But Laura felt deeply, warmly happy just the same. 'Good,' she said.

He smiled at her and leaned back. 'To get back to Bart for a minute. I believe in equality between men and women. But in the area of physical strength there's an obvious difficulty with a concept of equality. Bart is bigger than you. He could have done you harm. A woman is not behaving hysterically to remove herself from such a threat, even if the threat is nebulous. She's being sensible.'

'What if he comes looking for me?'

'Here, you mean? If he hasn't come yet, I shouldn't think it's likely—he's not totally lacking in intelligence.' He grinned. 'Anyway, don't worry. Aren't you always mightily impressed when I flex my muscles? Bart can't get past me.'

She had to laugh. Yet at the same time she felt both comforted and safe. Stifling a yawn, she rested her head on the arm of the chair and the flames danced in her eyes.

Charles said, 'You look worn out, Laura. I made up the spare bed for you.'

'Not sure I can walk that far,' she said drowsily.

'Is that a hint?'

Her eyes snapped open. 'No! Of course not.'

'Oh, come on. Allow me to be superior in this at least.' And he bent and picked her up, quilt and all.

She looped her arms around his neck and said against his chest, 'This is getting to be a habit.'

'And a very nice one. Although next time I think I should carry you to my bed, not this one.'

'Wonderful idea,' she murmured incautiously. 'Keep me away from the vodka, though.'

'We won't need vodka, Laura. We can get high on each other.'

Her very strict mother would not have approved of the way Laura kissed Charles on the mouth, said, 'So we can,' and then allowed herself to be tucked up in bed. It was just as dark outside as it had been in her own room earlier, and the rain was beating against the windows just as fiercely. But I'm safe with Charles, she thought, and on that thought fell asleep.

CHAPTER EIGHT

JULY slipped by, some days sunny, some foggy, some loud with rain and wind and the roar of the waves on the beach. For Laura the weather made no difference. Sun or rain, she was happy. And the major reason for her happiness was the man who lived in the cottage next door.

The morning after Bart's arrival Laura had walked back to her own cottage, nursing a hangover and a degree of trepidation. But Bart had gone. He had left the spare bed unmade—women are the ones who are supposed to make beds, Laura had thought sourly—and a letter on the table by the window. It was a bombastic letter with a legal flavour, containing sentences like, 'I was made to feel patently unwelcome,' 'I trust your good sense will prevail,' and 'I look forward to your early return.' Bart had not given up hope. Bart thought she was suffering from midsummer madness and would return to Grantham and dutifully assume the role of fiancée of the town lawyer. Bart, in other words, had not listened to a word she had said.

But the words had been said, and their effect, as Laura soon realised, was to liberate her from any lingering obligations to Bart. Although for three years she had drifted along in a kind of pseudo-intimacy that at the time had been enough, it had been an intimacy that could not stand the pressures of reality: the conflicts about money and the possibility of commitment. She was ashamed now to realise how shallow an intimacy it had been, and deeply relieved that it had never become a sexual intimacy.

The problem of Bart was resolved; Laura was gradually sorting out in her head and on paper (paper which she kept well-hidden) her various financial goals;

she was two-thirds the way through the organic chemistry text; and then there was Charles.

She saw him at least once a day, sometimes two or three times. They swam and walked on the beach, and in the evenings barbecued steaks or ate at Annie's, whose interest in the progress of their romance was avid. On rainy days they sat and read in front of the fire. They went to basketball games, Laura almost as happy as Charles on the evening of his team's first win. They went deep-sea fishing and lazed in the sun.

There were two things they did not do. They did not talk about Charles's background or family or job; and they did not make love.

They discussed any number of abstract subjects, ranging from the causes of aggression to the integrity of art. But Charles was adept at steering the conversation away from areas he did not want to discuss, so adept that Laura did not always realise what was happening.

As for the other, Charles kissed her occasionally and touched her only rarely. Yet Laura knew from the way he watched her, from the spark that could ignite his eyes, that he desired her. He was waiting, and although she did not know for what or why, she was content to have it so. For they were learning about each other. Becoming friends. At least friend was the word Laura used. She did not want to use that other word, love. She did not want to admit to herself that she might be falling in love with a man who in many ways was an enigma to her.

The occasion of Charles's birthday pointed out just how much of an enigma he was. Laura wanted his birthday to be an event. When they swam that morning she reminded him that he was invited for dinner and leaned across and kissed his salt-wet lips. 'Happy birthday,' she said.

'So you remembered.'

'Of course! Did you think I'd forget?'

He was busy rubbing himself with a towel. 'I guess not.'

'Charles Richards, look at me!' As he complied, grey eyes guarded, she went on more gently, 'I promised you I'd invite you for dinner on your birthday. I wouldn't forget that.'

'You're very sweet, Laura.'

'Sweet?' she said dubiously.

'Honest. Trustworthy. Fierce.' He gave her a lingering kiss. 'Soft. Yielding.' His second kiss left her with knees the consistency of a jellyfish; it seemed a very long time since he had kissed her that way. 'Passionate.'

Trying very hard to keep track of her wandering wits Laura said, 'And all that adds up to sweet?'

'I should also say caring, warm and generous. Sweet was obviously not an adequate word, was it?' Without the slightest change in inflection Charles added, 'I want to make love to you, Laura.'

'Now?' she gasped.

He smiled. 'Not in wet bathing suits on the sand, no. That kind of thing is all very well in fiction but damned uncomfortable in practice. But it's an issue we've avoided the last few days, isn't it? I don't want you to think that because I've been keeping my distance, I'm no longer interested. That's about as far from the truth as one could get.'

Laura wrapped her towel around her body, partly for the practical reason that she was cold, partly because her bikini suddenly seemed a woefully inadequate covering. She had no idea what to say.

He solved her dilemma. 'Do you want to make love to me, Laura?'

'You're different, Charles, I'll say that for you,' she responded warmly. 'Most men would ply me with wine and moonlight and roses before asking such a question. You do it in broad daylight when I'm cold and wet and my hair's a mess.'

'But this way I'll know you're not being swayed by the moonlight and the roses. I'll know your answer to be a true one.'

She looked at him through her lashes. 'Rational, not emotional?'

'Both,' he said firmly.

He had her cornered. And because she was a truthful woman, she raised her chin, looked him in the eye and said, 'Yes, I would like to make love with you.'

He took a step towards her, halted, and said helplessly, 'Laura . . . dearest Laura.'

She had never seen such blazing tenderness in a man's eyes before or felt such a surge of happiness and longing. For the first time she allowed herself to wonder if Charles was falling in love with her. He could not possibly know she had a million dollars; he would therefore love her for herself. Not until it had become a possibility did she realise just how badly she wanted it to happen.

Her hands were still clasping the towel to her breast. He took her left hand and brought it to his lips, pressing a kiss in the palm. His lips were cold, as cold as her skin; yet she did not think she could have been the recipient of a more beautiful gesture. She said weakly, 'We don't need moonlight and roses, do we?'

'No. I think that's what I was trying to tell you. Which is not to say that there's anything wrong with them.'

She said impulsively, 'Let's get dressed up this evening, Charles—make it an occasion. Will you wear a suit?'

'If you'll wear a dress.'

'Okay.' She laughed, still borne along on that surge of happiness. 'It'll be fun!'

'You're sure you don't want me to take you out for dinner, Laura? It doesn't seem fair for you to have all the work.'

'It's not work—I want to do it for you.'

He looked at a loss, unsure of his ground. 'You'll spoil me.'

As diplomatically as she could she said, 'Didn't your

mother bake birthday cakes for you, Charles? Make it a special day in some way?'

'She'd order the most expensive cake she could from the bakery. Not quite the same thing, as I'm sure you'd agree.'

Laura did agree, and wondered about all the things he had left unsaid as much as about what he had said. 'Would you prefer chocolate cake or an angel cake?'

'Chocolate.' He quirked his eyebrow. 'With lots of icing?'

'Done!'

He kissed her again with such mute gratitude that Laura felt like crying. 'What time's dinner?' he said.

'Seven o'clock.'

'I'll be there . . . thanks, Laura.'

He was thanking her for far more than a dinner invitation. 'My pleasure,' she said gravely. Then side by side they walked along the beach towards the cottages.

As the day progressed, Laura found that conversation much on her mind. Although she had meant every word when she had said she wanted to make love to Charles, she knew it to be a serious commitment on her part, one which frightened her with all its ramifications. Was it to be a two-week affair, brief as summer itself? Or was it to be seen as a reaching for a deeper intimacy, truly the making of love? She did not know how Charles would have answered those questions; and was almost afraid to look at her own answers.

She'd order the most expensive cake she could . . . Did that mean Charles's parents were wealthy? Or did it mean his mother was extravagant and not given to domesticity? If he came from a wealthy background why should he hide it? Or had something happened, a bankruptcy, a scandal, of which he was ashamed?

She could not believe he was hiding anything criminal. If he was, then her ability to judge people was totally out of kilter. Charles was straight, she'd swear. Somehow there was a simple explanation for his anger when she had overheard a 'phone call, for his reticence about his parents, for the three initials on the leather shaving kit ... what she was finding increasingly hurtful was his inability to trust her.

Her mind very much preoccupied with the possibility that she and Charles might make love that night, Laura drove into town. She went to the bank, the liquor store and the fish shop. She bought groceries. She spent a very long time in a card shop reading all the verses in the birthday cards, verses which either seemed too sentimental or too impersonal, finally settling on a card which depicted a couple walking along a beach hand in hand and which had a blank insert on which she could write whatever she liked.

She spent the entire afternoon puttering around the kitchen. She made lobster bisque, prepared the halibut for grilling and baked a rich two-layer chocolate cake, which she iced very generously once it was cool. She laid the table with new placemats and matching candles she had bought in town. She arranged paper, kindling and logs in the fireplace. Then she had a bath and put on the same sundress she had worn at Keltic Lodge.

She was nervous. Or was scared to death a more honest phrase, she wondered, applying rather too much eyeshadow to her right eyelid. She scrubbed it off and started again, aware that her hand was trembling. Get it together, Laura. You're not a virgin. You're not nineteen any more.

Unfortunately she felt as if she were both. She eventually produced identical mauve arcs on both lids and added eyeliner, not entirely straight. She got mascara on her nose as well as her lashes. Her lipstick, miracle of miracles, went on perfectly, and from a strategic distance from the mirror she looked poised and sophisticated. Charles won't notice the difference, she thought optimistically, choosing to ignore both his discernment and his sensitivity.

When he tapped at the door promptly at seven, she took off her apron, smoothed her hair and adopted a smile that she hoped combined a suitable warmth of welcome with a cool composure: a task that would not have been easy at the best of times. When she opened the door, however, the smile wavered and vanished, because Charles, looking extremely smart in a light summer suit, was holding out a huge bouquet of dark red roses. 'For you,' he said.

'B-but it's *your* birthday.'

'That doesn't matter.'

'But all I got you was a card.'

Over her shoulder he could see the carefully set table and to his nostrils must have drifted the delicious odour of the lobster bisque. 'You're giving me a great deal more than a card, Laura. Are you going to invite me in?'

'Of course,' she muttered, stepping back. He closed the door behind him, then put the bouquet in her arms. 'I can't produce a full moon,' he said lightly. 'But the roses I can manage.'

'They're beautiful,' she said, and so they were: dark, lustrous, each bloom perfectly shaped, petals curling. 'Charles, there must be two dozen of them. You'll be in the poorhouse.'

If this was, not very subtly, a probe, he avoided it. 'If I have to eat hamburger for the rest of the week it'll be worth it. From the look on your face you've never been given roses before.'

'A dozen once, when I was at university. But that's a long time ago ... I must put them in water.' Her nervousness had gone. She gave him a smile that was completely natural, kissed him on the lips and said happily, 'Thank you, Charles, they're lovely. Why don't you pour a couple of drinks while I'm finding a vase?'

After that, the evening went without a hitch. The bisque was piping hot, the halibut tender and moist, the vegetables pleasantly crisp. By the time they were ready for dessert, it was dark outside. Laura disappeared into the kitchen, lit the circle of candles on the cake and carried it into the living room, the tiny flames casting a circle of light on her face. Carefully she put the plate down in front of Charles. 'You have to make a wish before you blow out the candles,' she said.

He was staring at the cake. In white icing over the chocolate Laura had written *Happy Birthday, Charles*, the letters a little wobbly, but clearly recognisable.

'Charles? The wax is going to drip on the icing ... Charles, are you all right?'

'Yes,' he said in a strange voice, and blew out the candles. 'Yes, I'm fine.'

'You mustn't tell me what you wished or it won't come true.'

'I won't ... I can't yet, anyhow. Laura, come over here.' Uncertainly she walked towards him. He drew her head down and kissed her on the lips. 'Thank you. No one's ever made me a birthday cake before.'

He had brought the subject up. 'Why not?' she asked.

'Easier to buy one, I suppose.'

It was not the answer she had hoped for. 'Charles, are you ashamed of your family for some reason? I always have the feeling that you're hiding something, and I don't understand why.'

'No, I'm not ashamed, and hopefully before too long I can, as they say, reveal all,' he said flippantly. 'Until then I must ask you to be patient.'

She bit her lip. 'Don't you trust me?'

'Trust's got nothing to do with it ... pass me a knife and I'll cut you a piece of cake.'

Subject closed. She could not press him, for if she did he could throw into her face her own lack of openness; so she went to fetch a knife and in silence watched him cut the cake.

Although she protested, he insisted on helping her with the dishes after they had finished eating. In the crowded kitchen with Laura up to her wrists in suds and Charles wielding the dishtowel they recovered some of the easy intimacy of the first part of the evening. Then as Laura finished scouring the grillpan, the telephone rang. Anxiously she glanced at the clock. 'I hope nothing's wrong, I hate late-night calls.' Drying her hands as she went, she headed for the 'phone. 'Hello?'

'Laura—I'm on! Besicaglia wants me. Laura, the very best singing teacher in the country wants *me* as a student!'

'Keith, that's wonderful, dear! Congratulations!'

'He just called me five minutes ago. I had to let you know.'

'I'm so glad you did. Where are you?'

'Toronto. I go home tomorrow. I'm to start next month. It sounds like a ferocious schedule, but I'll be learning so much, and from the very best there is. I still can't believe it.'

She let him run on, deeply happy for him, yet knowing how much she would miss his steadiness and humour over the winter. Finally he said, 'There's one catch—he needs a deposit, and I haven't got enough.'

'No problem. Write a cheque and I'll 'phone tomorrow morning and transfer the money from my account.'

Across the hundreds of miles that separated them she could sense Keith's hesitation. 'I might have to ask for more money later on. I don't think I'll have the time to have a job over the winter.'

'That's no problem either, Keith. We'll talk about it when I get home. When do you actually go?'

'The middle of August. Laura, I swear I'll repay it all somehow. Every cent.'

'I'm sure you will,' she said, amused and touched by his independence. 'Keith, I'm so happy for you.'

'I knew you would be. That's why I 'phoned. I'm in a pay 'phone downtown and I haven't got any more change, I'd better go ... are you having a good time?' he added as a palpable afterthought. 'How's the man next door?'

'Wonderful,' she said, answering both questions. 'I'll call home in a couple of days and talk to you then.' They said goodbye and she hung up.

The design of the rooms was such that Charles must

have heard every word. She went back into the kitchen and said quickly, 'That was Keith. He's been accepted as a student of Besicaglia's in Toronto.'

'He must have a fine voice. Several of Besicaglia's students are singing at the Met. Laura, forgive me for being so direct, but how will you afford it? Besicaglia doesn't come cheap.'

'Keith has some money saved up.'

'Not enough for Besicaglia, I'd be willing to bet.'

'We'll work something out,' she said dismissively. 'Want some more coffee?'

'I have some contacts in Toronto. I'm sure I could find someone who'd sponsor Keith.'

If only she could say, I can afford it, I have lots of money. But she couldn't say that, and the reason she couldn't popped instantly into her head: she wanted Charles to say *I love you* without knowing about the money. She pulled her mind away from this disturbing train of thought—did she love Charles?—and said, 'Oh no, we couldn't do that.'

'Why not?'

She wrinkled her nose. 'Too much like charity.'

'The sponsorship of artists has been going on for hundreds of years.'

'Keith wouldn't take it, anyhow.'

'Keith may have to.'

She was growing angry. 'I asked if you wanted more coffee.'

'You're so damned independent!'

'Would you prefer me to be begging for handouts?' she snapped.

'I'd prefer you to be realistic.'

'You'd prefer me to do what you say!' She pulled out the oven door and shoved the grillpan inside in a clatter of metal.

'Laura——'

She had not finished. 'How do you think we managed the last four years? By going around with our hands out asking for help? Of course not. We worked, all of us.

The kids had paper rounds, Darren's had a job ever since he left school, Keith paid for all his university expenses, I worked at the hospital. And because we all worked, we darn well appreciated what we had. And don't say it—I know I'm old-fashioned and I believe in the work ethic and I'm out of step with the times. And if I've accomplished anything the last four years, I hope I've instilled the same beliefs in the kids—you pay as you go and you take responsibility for yourself.' She stood up slowly, recognising how afraid she had been when she had won the lottery that all this would change.

'So are you implying that I'm different?'

Her head snapped around, for there had been a real viciousness to his voice as if somewhere she had struck a raw nerve. 'I wasn't implying anything of the kind!' she retorted. 'How could I? I know nothing about your financial circumstances. Or about the way you were brought up. They're two of the subjects you refuse to discuss.'

He had taken off his jacket when he had joined her in the kitchen to clean up. Now he took it off the hook and put it on again. He was scowling. 'This isn't working out, is it?' he said. 'We're fighting over everything there is to fight about. I'd better go home.'

Laura stared at him, nonplussed. 'Why?' she burst out. 'Why are we fighting?'

He gave her a crooked smile. 'Because we're two essentially honest people who are attempting to deceive and not doing a very good job of it. That's one reason. Sexual frustration is probably the other. Nothing new about that, is there? But I don't think the mood is right to do anything about it.'

He sounded very definite. 'But it's your birthday!' she wailed ridiculously.

'I'll always remember the trouble you took, and the beautiful cake,' he said with obvious sincerity. 'Thank you, Laura.' He kissed her in the vicinity of her left cheekbone, said, 'I'll come by tomorrow morning to see if you want to go for a swim. Good night,' and left the room. The door clicked shut behind him and the screen door squeaked on its hinges. He was gone.

Laura, who despised weepy females, burst into tears.

She cried for several minutes, her face buried in her hands, her shoulders heaving, the evening in ruins about her. She had wanted so badly for his birthday to be perfect, an evening he would always remember. Oh, he'll remember it all right, she thought with a loud sniffle. But not for the reasons you hoped.

Weeping being a messy business, she eventually went to the bathroom, where she washed her face and blew her nose. You're in love with the man, she told her drooping reflection. Admit it, Laura. You're in love with Charles Richards.

Obscurely she was comforted. Among all the half-truths and evasions that seemed to hedge her in, that at least was a simple fact, one that had probably been staring her in the face for days. She grimaced at herself in the mirror. But now what? she thought ironically. She could ask him if he loved her, and if he said yes, she could tell him about the lottery. But if he said no . . . what then? If she were just an interesting summer diversion, a companion to swim with, a possible lover whom he would leave without a backward glance . . . how would she cope with that?

With a strange kind of detachment she watched the tears well up in her eyes again and spill over her lashes. In the autumn Charles would go back to Toronto to take up whatever life he led there, whereas she had to go back to Grantham: no choice for her. He would soon forget her. He might even be glad to see the last of her, a thought which literally terrified her.

She blew her nose again, checked the stove and turned out the lights, her eyes wincing away from the bouquet of dusky red roses. Her bedroom was very tidy, for she knew perfectly well she had been expecting the evening to end with Charles in her bed. Now, however, the clean sheets and the neatly arranged cosmetics on her bureau were a mockery; her aching body a reproach. The mood isn't right, Charles had said. He hadn't wanted her. That would be nearer the truth.

In a puerile fit of rage she threw her sandals across the room, flung her dress over the chair and fired her lacy underwear—worn with him in mind—after it. Naked, she climbed into bed, pulled the covers over her head and resolutely closed her eyes.

She did not want to be alone. Oh God, how she wanted him here beside her, his hands on her body, his passion engulfing her so that they forgot everything but their need of each other.

Sitting up, she pounded her pillow into a more amenable shape, then lay down again. Hormones, she thought fiercely. This is all a matter of hormones. As if the biochemistry text was open in front of her, she listed them off: FSH, LH and LTH, progesterone, estrone, estradiol and estriol. She mentally tabulated all their properties; she reviewed their various functions in the female body.

It didn't help. Her hormones were no doubt in a turmoil and part of her misery was simply physical need. But if that were all, Bart would do just as well as Charles. Her flesh cringed from the thought of Bart in her bed. I want Charles. I need Charles. I love Charles . . . Giving the tangled covers a good kick, she decided that she sounded like a crooner bewailing her star-crossed fate. That didn't help either.

The bedside clock ticked away the minutes. The waves sang their rhythmic, ineffective lullaby on the beach. Laura drank a glass of water, counted sheep, tried to read a mystery that at any other time would have entertained her, and at two-forty-five fell asleep over chapter twelve of Reinhold, Smith and Beakston *Organic Chemistry*.

CHAPTER NINE

FIVE and a half hours later Charles was standing in the doorway of Laura's bedroom. He was wearing a swimsuit and had his towel draped over one shoulder. He had knocked on the door. No response. He had opened the door and called Laura's name, with a similar lack of response. After a brief hesitation he had stepped inside. His bare feet soundless on the floor, he had crossed the living room. And now he was at the door of her room.

The room told its own tale. Clothes rumpled on the chair, bedside light still burning even though dimmed by the morning sun, two books at the foot of the bed where the bedding was pulled away from the mattress. He knew Laura was in the bed because of the hump under the covers, but all he could see of her was a sprig of dark hair between the pillows.

Charles was not a man used to expressing the gentler emotions. Irresolutely he stayed by the door, knowing what would happen if he went into the room. Then his eyes caught another detail: two crumpled tissues on the floor beside the bed. Laura had been crying.

It was all he needed. He draped the towel over the doorknob, walked over to the bed, sat down on the edge and rested a hand on the huddled form under the quilt. 'Laura?' he said, a tentative note in his voice that might have surprised some of his Toronto acquaintances.

Under his hand he felt the slow rise and fall of her breathing. Other than that, she did not stir. He increased the pressure of his hand, 'Laura, wake up.'

Laura had been dreaming. She was to meet Charles after a basketball game. But her car wouldn't start, and when she hitched a ride in a transport truck the driver insisted on taking her for dinner at Annie's. They ate halibut and birthday cake, and then Archie drove her all the way to the high school on the wrong side of the road. But when they arrived, Charles was gone. The black-jacketed young man who had accosted her in the alley put his arm around her, telling her to wake up. She mumbled accusingly, 'He didn't wait,' then suddenly realised the hand and the voice were real.

She sat up in a flurry of bare breasts, grabbed the sheet and pulled it to her chin, and said, 'What are you doing here?'

Charles smiled into her startled brown eyes. 'Waiting for you to wake up.'

For a horrified moment she thought he was as naked as she. Then she saw his swimsuit, and the towel on the door. 'I am *not* going for a swim this morning,' she announced.

He turned off the bedside lamp. With one finger he traced the blue shadows under her eyes. 'You didn't sleep well.'

'I—no.'

'Neither did I.'

Laura would have felt in a much stronger position strategically if she had been wearing a nightgown and if he was not exposing quite so much bare flesh. 'Oh,' she said inanely.

His smile widened. His eyes were full of warmth, without guile. 'I wanted to be where I am now,' he said, and leaned forward and kissed her sleep-softened mouth.

It was a slow, languorous kiss with infinite possibilities. Laura felt almost as if she were dreaming again. Charles had been waiting for her and they were together as they should be. His hands reaching to cup her face were part of the dream, as was their slow slide to her shoulders. As she felt the first touch of his tongue and opened to him, the golden radiance of the sun became her own happiness, the singing of the birds the singing of her heart.

She had been clasping the sheet to her chin. She let go of it, letting her palms reach out for his hair-roughened chest. He made a tiny sound in his throat and took the softness of her breasts in his hands. He must have felt the shock ripple through her body; against her mouth he murmured, 'Laura, do you want me to stop?'

She knew in her bones if she asked him to stop, he would; nothing would be done against her will. She did not want him to stop. She nibbled gently at his lips, holding him more strongly. 'I'm very happy,' she said.

He needed no other answer. He pushed her back against the pillows, kissing her ever more deeply, while his impatient hands pulled aside the quilt that covered her. When he lay down beside her he discovered her nakedness. Laura heard his indrawn rasp of breath as his fingers travelled her flesh in incredulous discovery, and she abandoned shyness for joy and caution for generosity. She had swum with this man and lain on the beach beside him, but neither had prepared her for the smoothness of his skin, for its warmth, for the tautness of muscle and the rigidity of bone that lay beneath, for the clean yet undeniably masculine scent of his body. She sensed him pulling at the drawstring of his swimsuit, then in an expression of wonder felt against her, tangibly, all his desire. In an instinct as old as time she opened her thighs to him, wanting him so fiercely and with such passionate need that all subtlety fled. Delay was unbearable; prolongation an agony beyond imagining. She wanted him now. She had to have him now.

She arched her back, felt him plunge within her and cried aloud in pleasure and in a torment of longing. His head was at her breast, his hips moving in unison with her own as if they had done this together many times before; she wrapped her legs around his and thrust her body against him and gave herself up to the blinding, glorious rhythms. Deaf to her own cries, she was aware only of their joined convulsion, of the pounding of his heart against her ribs as they fell through the tiny death that is fulfilment into the exhausted peace beyond.

Outside the birds were still crazily singing in the sunshine and the waves still fell on the grey sand ... how could that be, thought Laura, when so much else had changed? She closed her eyes, cherishing the exquisite peace that had followed the frenzy of their coupling. Her lips were resting against Charles's throat. With lazy sensuality she stroked his shoulder, tracing the hard arc of his collarbone and the soft flesh in the hollow beneath. 'That was beautiful,' she murmured.

He nuzzled his mouth into her neck. 'Beautiful is scarcely the word ... earth-shattering is more like it. Laura, my sweet, when I thought of making love to you—and I might as well admit I've been thinking of very little else lately—I planned to take my time, to be as slow as I could, to give you all the pleasure I was capable of. What do the books call it? Foreplay.' He raised his head and she saw beneath the tenderness and satiation in his face a trace of anxiety. 'Instead of which I totally lost control. I wanted you so badly, I couldn't wait.'

Quickly, before he could say more, she pressed a finger to his mouth. 'Are you suggesting you're the only one who lost control? I was in just as much of a hurry as you were, Charles—and was, I am sure, equally fulfilled.'

She watched the anxiety disappear, to be replaced by a smile of complicity. 'Next time we could be more—er, leisurely.'

She gave a deliciously naughty chuckle. 'You're already talking about next time?'

He moved one hand to her breast and circled it very slowly. 'It's not just talk, dearest Laura.'

Love for him flooded her body with sweetness. She bit back the words and said pertly, 'I thought we were going swimming.'

'Swimming can wait. This can't.

His lips were following the course of his fingers. With deliberate delicacy she began tracing the contours of his chest, her hands moving ever lower, her body boneless with the rebirth of desire; and this time it did take considerably longer before they lost control.

Afterwards, they slept. Laura woke first, to find herself in the circle of Charles's arms, his breath soft on her cheek, his body curved protectively around hers. The birds were quiet, the sun no longer beamed in the window. By very cautiously moving her head, she saw that it was early afternoon. She decided with absolute certainty that she was happier than she had ever been in her life, and, on a more mundane level, that she was extremely hungry.

She ran her fingers up and down Charles's spine. Without opening his eyes, he said, 'You stop that. Twice in one morning is enough for any woman.'

'It's afternoon,' she said innocently, tickling his ribs.

He grabbed her in a bear hug and squeezed her until she was giggling helplessly. 'I'm the boss around here,' he growled.

She touched him in a very suggestive place and fluttered her lashes at him. 'Oh?'

Charles began to laugh. 'I must be a miserable failure as a lover—you're never satisfied!'

'You're not a failure at all—you're so good, I keep on wanting more. But——' she pushed her palms against his chest, 'I'd also like some breakfast. Or lunch. Or whatever.'

'Rejected for bacon and eggs. Sounds like a great idea.'

He sat up, running his fingers through his hair and letting his eyes linger on the shadowed curves of her body. When she glanced up and saw his expression, she blushed as fierily as if they had exchanged none of the intimacies of the past few hours. The only words that would have matched his expression were—I love you. He did not say them; neither, therefore, did she. She did say prosaically, conquering the urge to hide behind the sheet, 'Do you want the bathroom first? There are towels in the cupboard.'

'Okay.' He reached over and touched her cheek, his voice deepening. 'Thank you, Laura—you were wonderful.' And with that she had to be content.

Laura was reasonably receptive to other people's feelings, and had she seen Charles behaving with another woman as he was behaving with her she would have said he was in love. He was a sensitive and inventive lover as well as an intuitive companion, and as the days of her holiday began to rush by, she sang about the cottage and laughed more than she had ever laughed in her life before and made love fiercely, wantonly, and with an open-hearted generosity that he more than matched. But, for all this, Charles did not speak of his feelings, nor did he speak of the future.

Laura had talked by telephone to Keith, who was home now, working at two jobs and saving every cent he earned and still deliriously happy; she had also spoken to Sue-Ann who was still entranced with Steven, something of a record for her. Darren, according to Sue-Ann, was liking his job at the dairy-farm. 'It's the first time he's worked with animals,' said Sue-Ann shrewdly. 'I think it's good for him—he likes them better than people. He's certainly been a lot nicer to have around since he got that job.'

'Maybe he's nicer because I'm away,' said Laura wryly.

'No, that's not it,' Sue-Ann answered seriously. 'He even asked how you were and said to say hello. I'm sure you'll see a difference when you get home. He's not as—scratchy.'

'I hope you're right . . . you sound tired, Sue-Ann.'

'I didn't feel very well today. There's a 'flu bug at the hospital, I've probably picked it up. Surely nurses must eventually get immune to things like the 'flu?'

'One would think so. Take care of yourself, won't you? How's the housekeeper working out?'

'Well, she's all right. I'll be glad when you're home, though.'

Laura was not immune to being needed. 'Bless your heart!' she said. 'I'll call again in a couple of days, Sue-Ann. Be sure and say hello to Darren for me.' And they rang off.

If it were not for the dilemma of Charles, Laura would have been looking forward to going home. But the thought of leaving him filled her with panic. Her feelings for him compared to her feelings for Bart were like the sun compared to the moon: the latter a pale reflection of the former. She had to believe that Charles was as aware as she of that burning radiance when they were together. If he was not, then she was no judge of human nature.

Your judgment was off as far as Bart was concerned. It could be off again, a nasty little voice whispered in her ear.

Get lost, she responded pithily. We learn from our mistakes. And Charles is different.

Then, swiftly, a week before she was due to go home, Laura made two discoveries that coalesced all her doubts. The first, of necessity, she had to keep to herself.

She had spent the night in Charles's bed. He was in the bathroom, showering; she was standing dreamily by the bedroom window, looking out at a grey, foggy day with a fatuous smile on her face. She was wearing a robe of his, and as she turned away from the window the wide sleeve caught a pile of magazines on the bureau so that three or four of them slithered to the floor. She bent to pick them up. They were copies of a local news magazine that originated in Halifax. Idly she flipped through last month's issue. On one of the pages at the very back, in a section devoted to advertising, her own face looked up at her.

Her heart lurched. Small black-and-white photographs of the lottery winners were arranged in the lower right-hand corner of the page, and while the photograph of herself was not a particularly good one and her hair was longer than it now was, she was nevertheless entirely recognisable. Her name and her home town were printed underneath.

Had Charles seen the photograph? If he had, then he would have known right from the beginning that she was a wealthy woman, a millionairess. A good catch. Had his queries about her home town and the cost of Keith's singing lessons been motivated by more than ordinary curiosity? Had he been probing, trying to ascertain for certain that she was indeed a rich woman? And if, as she had suspected, there had been some kind of financial scandal or bankruptcy in his family—for she had always sensed he had a privileged, if not a wealthy background—then how welcome would be her arrival on the scene!

The shower had turned off. She heard Charles singing in the bathroom, not nearly as melodiously as Keith could sing. Hurriedly she shoved the magazines to the bottom of the pile and began to make the bed, anything to keep herself occupied so she would not have to think. By the time Charles emerged from the bathroom, his hair still wet, his hips swathed in a towel, she was in the kitchen busily making coffee.

He came up behind her and kissed her on the neck. 'Morning, gorgeous,' he said. 'Bed made, coffee on— you're being very domesticated.'

Laura had managed not to start at the touch of his lips. But her body was rigid and her voice a little higher pitched than usual when she replied, 'You get to make the pancakes.' She reached up for mugs, not looking at him. 'Then I must go home. I told you I finished reviewing the organic chemistry, didn't I? I want to get a good start on some biology before I leave.'

'Lots of chemistry and biology right here,' he murmured, putting his arms around her waist and pulling her back against his chest. 'Put the mugs down,

Laura, and give me a kiss. I haven't had one for half an hour.'

'Poor you,' she mocked, wondering if she sounded as brittle as she felt.

Charles had been absently smoothing the flatness of her belly. His hands stilled. 'Is something wrong?'

'No . . . what could be wrong?'

'Look at me.' He turned her body in his arms. He was frowning. 'What's up, Laura? Something's wrong . . .'

With what she still felt had been adequate motives Laura had embarked on a single deception in her relationship with Charles: that of her financial status. But she had since learned how one deception leads to another, until she was enmeshed in half-truths and evasions. She rested her face against his throat, thereby avoiding his eyes, and said, 'I'm tired, that's all. I didn't get much sleep last night—remember?'

'You seem edgy . . . tense.'

His choice of words was dead on, she thought grimly. 'Maybe all I need is my caffeine fix,' she said with a flippancy she could tell he did not appreciate.

'I wonder sometimes what we really know about each other,' he said soberly. 'Each of us is keeping secrets, we know that. Who's going to be the first to tell, Laura? You or me? Trouble is, I'm waiting for you and you're probably waiting for me.'

He was painfully near the truth. Tell me you love me, she wanted to cry. And tell me also you haven't read that magazine. She moved his hands from her waist and poured the coffee. 'I expect it will all work out,' she said with a confidence she was far from feeling.

He added his usual overdose of sugar to his coffee and stirred it moodily. 'Yeah,' he said. But he did not sound convinced.

Laura showered while Charles made pancakes; she had discovered in the time that she had known him that he was an erratic cook, producing meals that were interesting if not always easily digestible. But he was justifiably proud of his pancakes. She doused them with butter and syrup and poured another cup of coffee, noticing that uncertainty did not seem to have harmed her appetite, and all the while she chattered on about some of the ups and downs of being a surrogate parent for three teenagers. She did not, however, deceive Charles, who said as she got up to leave, 'Great smoke screen, Laura.'

She glowered at him. 'Was I boring you?'

'You've never yet done that—in bed or out.'

'Oh, go to hell,' she said irritably.

'That's one choice. Or we could go to Louisbourg instead,' he said unexpectedly. 'It's a wonderful evocative place in the fog.'

'To the fortress, you mean?' She had not yet been there.

'Yes. We could walk to the shore, the surf's always impressive.'

'I should study.'

'I'll pick you up at two. That'll give you three hours.'

When he smiled like that, she couldn't resist him. Please God, don't let him know about the million dollars. 'All right. Two o'clock it is.'

The intricate architecture and bizarre sex lives of the microscopic protozoans failed to hold Laura's attention. She was heartily glad when Charles came to pick her up and had resolved to put the photographs in the magazine out of her mind. When she thought back she realised the magazine had seemed in mint condition, which would indicate Charles had almostly certainly not read it. After all, if he had seen the photograph he would have asked her about it. Wouldn't he?

Fog enveloped the little town of Louisbourg, which smelled strongly of fish. 'That hasn't changed,' Charles said cheerfully. 'In the 1700s they used to dry the split cod on flakes in the sun. Cod was the gold of the eighteenth century—an absolute necessity in a Catholic country ... Talking about absolute necessities, I'd better stop and get some gas.'

He pulled into a gas station, drew up by the pumps and asked for unleaded and an oil check. Then he pulled out his wallet, partially extracting a couple of notes. 'That should cover it. I've got to look after another absolute necessity.' Whistling, he strode in the direction of the washrooms.

Laura was smiling. In his dark blue cords and yellow windbreaker Charles looked very ordinary: no figure of romance, no breaker of hearts. Why was she so drawn to him? Why in the wild tumult of their lovemaking did she want to cry I love you? Why, afterwards, in the peace of his embrace, did she want to whisper the same three words?

I want him to be happy. I want him to trust me, to let down all the barriers. I want him to love me.

She picked up his wallet as the attendant slammed the hood and called, 'Only down half a litre. That's twenty-six dollars, ma'am.'

She gave him thirty dollars. An inner leather flap in the wallet had fallen open, revealing Charles's driver's licence in a transparent plastic sleeve. Her eyes flicked over it, then stopped, riveted. The printed black letters said Charles Richard Thorndyke. Her brain instantly made the connection. C.R.T. The initials on the shaving kit. Charles's name was not Charles Richards, as he had said. It was Charles Richard Thorndyke.

'Your change, ma'am,' the attendant repeated, holding out two two-dollar notes. 'You okay?'

Laura gaped at him, accepting the money and shoving it into the note compartment. 'Yes. Yes, I'm fine. Thanks.' Then she saw Charles coming around the corner of the building. She fastened the leather flap, hiding the licence from view, and dropped the wallet on to the driver's seat as if it were burning her fingers.

Charles stopped to chat with the attendant, who was admiring the Jeep. She drew several long, slow breaths, trying to slow the sick pounding of her heart. Charles had been using an assumed name ever since she had met him. But *why*? What in God's name had he done that he

had to hide from her his true identity? Thorndyke ...
she racked her brains, trying to remember if she had
ever seen the name in newspaper articles or magazines,
or heard it on the radio. But she drew a complete blank.
Nothing. The name meant nothing to her. At least he's
not a mass murderer, she thought with a desperate kind
of humour. I'd have heard about him if he was. A
thought which brought no comfort.

Her hands were cold. She shoved them in the pockets
of her jeans. The two men had gone around the back of
the Jeep, where she could hear the rumble of their
voices without being able to distinguish any words. She
practised a couple of smiles; her face muscles were stiff.

From the cadence of the voices she could tell that the
conversation at the back of the Jeep was coming to an
end. She drew another long breath, trying to relax her
clenched knuckles. Then Charles was opening the door,
laughing at some joke of the attendant's. He looked
young and carefree as his smile slipped over to include
Laura. She produced the smile she had practised and
saw to her surprise that he noticed nothing amiss. He
put the wallet in his back pocket and snapped his seat
belt. 'Hope you didn't mind waiting a few minutes.
That fellow's interested in buying one of these things, so
he wanted to know how I liked it.'

'No, I didn't mind,' Laura said. Her voice not only
worked, it sounded perfectly natural.

They turned back on the highway, which curved to
the left along the shoreline. The last of the houses
disappeared. The fog billowed in from the sea, clothing
in moisture the scrub spruce, which was bent by the
ocean winds, and the tall white-flowered plants that
stood straight as soldiers in the grass.

'Angelica,' said Charles. 'The French brought it over
here for their herb gardens, and now it grows wild all
around the fortress. A born survivor.' He turned up a
dirt road. 'We have to park the Jeep and go out to the
fortress in a bus. Try and blank out all the tourists and
picture it as it was.'

From brochures at the Information Centre Laura gained a quick overview of the history of the fortress, which during its brief lifespan of forty years had been twice besieged and had twice fallen; it was blasted to the ground by the British in 1760 and lay buried for over two hundred years, its grass-covered ruins a grazing place for sheep and deer. But in its heyday it had been a centre for commerce and fishing, a naval and military base, home for as many as five thousand people from artisans to aristocrats, and prostitutes to Sisters of the Congregation of Notre Dame.

While burying her nose in the brochures meant Laura did not have to talk to Charles, it also kindled in her a very genuine interest in what she was about to see. As the bus crossed the causeway and she saw ahead of her the drawbridge at the Porte Dauphine, surmounted by a royal crest and guarded by a uniformed sentry, she felt a quiver of excitement.

Nor did the fortress fail her. She wandered entranced through the streets, Charles pointing out the landmarks: the cone-shaped ice house; the barracks, once the largest building in New France, topped by a slender, graceful tower where a clock ticked away the minutes of a more modern century; the imposing home of the engineer; the bakery; the guardhouse; the inn by the waterfront where privateers and fishermen would have roistered and sung; the peaceful, formal gardens where vegetables and herbs had been grown to supplement a diet that at best must have been tedious. Chickens scratched and clucked around a fisherman's house, built *en picquet*. A cow lowed behind the barracks. The guards marched past in a rattle of drums.

Charles had already asked if Laura wanted to go inside some of the buildings. She had declined, content to absorb the atmosphere of the town with its grey buildings, grey fog, grey sea. She caught glimpses of women in long woollen skirts and men in chemises, of a child in wooden shoes; she almost expected to see a French warship at anchor in the mist and hear the creak of its rigging. When she and Charles passed beyond the site of the reconstruction to the flat grassy plain where the rest of the town had stood, she looked back and saw what other eyes, over two hundred years ago, would have seen: the angled solidity of rooflines, the comforting cluster of buildings, the walls and ramparts to keep out the invader and enclose this tiny pocket of humanity so far from home.

In silence she walked at Charles's side down the straight dirt track that passed the foundations of the hospital, one of the first in North America, and cut between the heaped-up ruins of the old city wall. They were in the wilderness now, the bog, no-man's land, where the surf roared and the seagulls cried out their loneliness to the four winds.

Once again Laura turned to face the fortress. But it had disappeared as if it had never been, swallowed by the fog. She felt the damp air bite through her clothes and shivered from more than the cold.

'So you feel it, too,' Charles said softly. 'I thought you would.'

She looked at him in silence, seeing a tall, blond-haired man whose body she had come to know almost as well as her own yet whose eyes were the opaque grey of the fog. 'The sense of impermanence,' he went on in the same quiet voice. 'Of human striving that comes to nought. Of wars that mean nothing to us today, for they have been replaced by other wars. Of people who ate and drank and made love, and now lie in forgotten graves.'

She knew exactly what he meant. That she should be so spiritually attuned to a man who had lied about his identity, that most basic of concepts, seemed the height of irony. She found she had nothing to say.

'Do you want to walk along the wall for a while? We might get lucky and find some kind of an artefact—even a musketball.'

She could tell Charles wanted to walk along the wall, that he had some of a small boy's excitement at the thought of finding a fragment from the past, and without warning pain ripped through her because she loved him so much. Gazing vaguely over her shoulder, she said, 'You go along the wall—I think I'd rather walk to the shore. I'll meet you back here in half an hour.' Not giving him the chance to argue, she turned away and loped across the grass towards the sea, where the boulders were blurred by the fog and by the tears crowding her eyes. Charles did not follow her. When she reached the foam-spewed boundary of land and sea, she risked a backwards glance. He was heading towards the wall, his yellow jacket a bright note of colour in a landscape made up of greys and greens.

Pulling up the hood of her windbreaker Laura tramped along the shore. She should tell Charles what she had discovered: common sense dictated that she should. There might conceivably be a simple explanation, although she could not imagine what it would be, which would obliterate her anguished sense of betrayal and, deeper, her anger. But at the same time she knew she would not tell him. Not often did she think of herself as cowardly; but in this matter her fear of what she might find out was paralysing her into inaction.

One thing she could do. When she got back to Grantham (how quickly she had come to think of the cottage as home), she could go to the university library and check the name Thorndyke in the newspaper files. The name must in some way be crucial for Charles to have kept it hidden from her. In the name must lie the solution to the mystery.

But she was not yet due to return to Grantham. Somehow, in the meantime, she had to act naturally with Charles, laugh and talk and—she flinched—make love as if nothing had happened.

As she kept walking, already out of breath from clambering over the wet, slippery rocks, imperceptibly her spirit was soothed by the clean, cold smell of the sea and the unceasing thunder of waves and foam. Panting, she stopped for a minute, looking around her.

A chaos of water to her left, bounded by the blank, grey fog; the hillocks of a peat bog to her right. She knew that the first besiegers of the fortress, a ragged band of ill-armed New Englanders, had dragged their cannon across that bog, and that their shouts of jubilation and the music of their pipes had sounded across the marsh when they had breached the ramparts and taken the town: an astonishing victory, which the fortress itself had revenged, for over nine hundred of the New Englanders had died that first winter, living and dead lying together in the cold, damp barracks.

Laura gave herself a shake. Enough of death and destruction, she thought, glancing at her watch and realising that she should have met Charles five minutes ago. One effect of the great grey fortress was to make time seem irrelevant. Briefly she considered taking a short cut across the bog, but the prospect of being alone on its unmarked wastes did not appeal to her; so she set out along the shoreline, travelling with guilty haste. She had gone farther than she had intended.

She heard Charles before she saw him. He was shouting her name, the two syllables floating eerily in the fog, disembodied as a ghost. Catching her breath, she called, 'Here! Over this way!'

She waited for a minute, hearing the rocks rattle like bones and the surf roar like cannons. Charles could be within twenty feet of her and walk past without seeing her, so thick was the fog ... 'Charles!' she yelled in sudden panic. 'Charles, where are you?'

'Lau-ra!'

Further away. Ahead of her, or to her left? She could not tell. Not knowing which way to go, she stayed where she was, feet braced against the rocks. She could not possibly get lost, because if she followed the shoreline she would eventually arrive at the fortress, which was a comforting thought to hold on to. But what if Charles had passed her and was even now going in the opposite direction, away from her rather than towards her? What if he slipped on the rocks and broke an ankle? What if he took to the marsh rather than staying on the shore?

She took a deep breath, cupped her hands around her mouth and shouted his name as loudly as she could.

Footsteps scraped on the rocks. She would not have been surprised to see an unshaven soldier in a baggy homespun uniform emerge from the mist. Instead she saw a yellow jacket and blue cords. A twentieth-century man, flesh and blood, undeniably real.

Charles strode towards her, his hands in his pockets, his hair dark with moisture. Oh dear, Laura thought, not really surprised. He's angry.

Her first words left no doubt of it. 'Where the *devil* have you been?'

'Walking along the shore. Soaking up the atmosphere.'

'Spare me the puns. You were supposed to be back half an hour ago.'

'I'm sorry,' she said with complete honesty. 'I lost track of the time.'

'I thought you were lost. Do you realise how long you could wander around on these marshes without anyone finding you?'

'Credit me with enough intelligence to have stayed by the shore,' she retorted, deciding not to tell him that she had indeed contemplated a short cut over the bog.'

'You could have broken an ankle on the rocks.'

'So could you. Charles, I've said I'm sorry. I'm not going to say it again.'

'You're so goddamned independent!'

He had stepped closer. The slab of granite on which he was standing was three or four inches above her own foothold, forcing her to crane her neck upwards. She said coldly, 'We both know you're bigger than me.'

'Maybe it's time I proved it.'

What she saw in his eyes made Laura take two quick steps backwards. But her heel caught in a crevice. She twisted to keep her balance and ended up with her behind plunked on a large boulder that the sea had not eroded sufficiently to make it a comfortable landing place. Her cheeks scarlet, her dignity as sorely tried as her posterior, she said furiously, 'I'm not in the mood for he-man stuff. I'm cold and wet and I want to go home.'

Unceremoniously Charles hauled her to her feet. 'That's fine with me, I was ready to go home half an hour ago. Follow me and for God's sake don't go wandering off.'

His fingers were digging into her wrist. She said tightly, 'If I pushed you into the sea, do you think they'd call it justifiable homicide?'

For the first time there was a flash of genuine amusement in his face. 'They'd call it temporary insanity. Because you haven't got a hope of succeeding.'

'Oh, you have an answer for everything!' she raged. 'Let go of my wrist, I'm not a child that you have to pull along behind you. I'm a grown woman who's managed to look after herself for twenty-five years—a fact you often seem to forget.'

The amusement was open now. 'They say the devil looks after his own.'

'Very funny. Get moving.'

He bent and kissed her full on the mouth, grinned at her flushed, outraged face and said, 'You look very beautiful when you're angry. Almost as beautiful as you look after you make love.' Then he dropped her wrist, turned his back and headed back the way they had come.

Laura contemplated throwing a tantrum or going in the opposite direction; but the thought of the cottage, dry clothes and a cup of tea restrained her. She walked along behind Charles, and as she went could acknowledge to herself that losing her temper with him had camouflaged the deeper hurt that stemmed from his deception. Hopefully now she would not blurt out that she knew his real name and that he had been systematically lying to her. Sooner or later she supposed she would have to confront him. Later sounded the more attractive option.

They reached the grassy clearing and trudged along the dirt track, re-entering the confines of the old fortress. The huddled buildings took form through the mist, watched over by the thin spire on the barracks and the crenellated ramparts. The tourists also reappeared, hung about with cameras, yelling at children, complaining about the weather. The bus seemed totally incongruous; how the soldiers would have gawked at it! She and Charles got on board and were driven off the peninsula and up the hill to the car park. The shrouded stones of the fortress had disappeared.

Laura buckled herself into the seat of the Jeep, rested her head against the window and closed her eyes, partly because she was tired, partly because she did not want to talk to Charles. By the time they left the town of Louisbourg she was asleep, a fitful sleep in which grey-coated soldiers on the turrets fired loaves of bread at her that were as hard as cannonballs, and a bewigged aristocrat imperiously seated on the clock tower kept moving the gold hands of the clock so that she was always too late . . . too late.

She woke up with a start and saw the cottage in front of her, an ordinary, modern cottage with very little past and no ghosts that she knew of. 'Oh. We're here.'

'May I come in?'

'I'd rather you didn't,' she babbled. 'I don't really——'

'I left my mac here a couple of days ago. If I could get it, then I'll leave you in peace. I can take a hint, Laura.'

Her descent from the Jeep was a blatant retreat from the anger and pain in Charles's eyes. She hurried up the steps and unlocked the door, and heard the shrill peal of the telephone.

She had the sensation it had already rung more than once. She ran across the room, leaving a trail of wet footsteps behind her, and grabbed the receiver off the hook. 'Hello,' she said breathlessly.

'Laura! It's Keith. I've been trying to reach you all afternoon.'

'Why? What's wrong?'

'It's okay—everything's going to be okay. But Sue-Ann's down with the 'flu and Darren was admitted to hospital this afternoon, they're operating for appendicitis.'

Laura's knuckles were white on the receiver. 'You mean they're operating right now?'

'Yes. They say there's no cause for concern, it hasn't perforated, just routine surgery. But I knew you'd want to know.'

'Oh, yes! And Sue-Ann?'

'A good old-fashioned case of stomach 'flu. Poor kid, she looks like a ghost. I'm home with her right now, then Jane's coming over later to stay with her while I go over to the hospital. Just to add to the confusion the housekeeper got the chance for a trip to Boston a couple of days ago, so she upped and quit.'

'I'll come home right away.'

'You don't have to, Laura——'

'Of course I do—I have to see Darren. There wasn't any warning, was there, Keith?'

'Well, you know Darren. The last thing he'd admit to was being in pain. I thought he looked a bit drawn the last few days, but I put it down to his new job. The hours are crazy, he starts at five a.m.'

'Look, I'll start home right away. I'll probably go straight to the hospital before I come to the house. If you see Darren and he's in any shape for a message, tell him I'm coming and give him my love.'

'You drive carefully. It's late to be starting out.'

'I will, I promise. Give Sue-Ann my love as well.'

'Okay. See you later, Laura.'

'Bye.' She put down the receiver and stared blankly at the wall.

'What's wrong, Laura?'

She had forgotten Charles's presence. 'Darren's got appendicitis, they're operating now. And Sue-Ann's got the 'flu. That was Keith.' She looked around distractedly. 'I'm going home—I've got to pack.'

'You're leaving now?'

'I have to. I can't leave Keith to cope, he's holding down two jobs.' She looked around the room. 'Oh Lord, where will I begin?'

'I'll help,' Charles said promptly. 'Where are your suitcases?'

By going from room to room picking up everything that was hers and throwing it in the nearest suitcase, Laura got packed in an astonishingly short time. She stripped the bed, then said helplessly, 'What'll I do with the sheets and towels? I don't want to leave used ones behind—and the refrigerator, it's full of food.'

'Don't worry—when I get back, I'll clean out the refrigerator and take the bedding to the laundromat.'

'Would you? That would be such a help.' Then the rest of his words sank in and she gazed at him in perplexity. 'What do you mean . . . when you get back?'

Charles looked down at her. 'I'm coming with you, Laura. You don't think I'd let you start out at this hour of the day by yourself? We'll have to take your car, of course. I can fly back——'

'No!' she gasped. 'No, you can't come.' If he went to Grantham he would find out about the million dollars; inevitably he would find out. She remembered the magazine and added inwardly, *unless he already knows* . . .

'Laura, for God's sake——'

'You can't!' she said wildly.

He made a visible effort to control himself. 'Look, I understand that we're going home to your family. Naturally, we won't sleep together, you can trust me to be discreet.'

Sleeping arrangements had been the last thing on her mind. 'That's got nothing to do with it. Charles, please don't give me a hard time. I'll be perfectly all right driving home on my own and I'll call you tomorrow morning to let you know how everyone is.'

The very reasonableness of her tone appeared to infuriate Charles. 'Are you ashamed of me?' he snarled. 'Ashamed of our relationship? So you want to keep me out of sight of your family?'

'Don't be ridiculous!' she stormed, thought of his hidden identity, dropped her eyes and finished lamely, 'Why should I be ashamed?'

'I don't know. You tell me.'

She made one last valiant effort. 'Charles, you're over-reacting. I'm a good driver who's entirely capable of travelling four hundred miles on her own. There's no necessity for you to go with me. Besides, the airport's over a hundred miles from where we live, it's not just a simple matter of you walking out of the back door and getting on a plane there.'

'Where *do* you live, Laura?' His voice was dangerously quiet. 'And why won't you tell me? What are you hiding?'

Inside her something snapped. She said venomously, 'At least I've given you my real name.'

His eyes narrowed. 'What do you mean?'

'*I'm* not using a false identity. My name is my real name. What are *you* hiding, Charles Richard Thorndyke?'

He paled and grabbed her sleeve. 'How long have you known?'

'So you don't deny it?' Against all logic Laura had been cherishing the hope that there was a simple explanation, that Charles had not wilfully deceived her.

'*How long have you known?*'

She raised her chin, not allowing herself to flinch away from eyes that pierced her like sharpened steel. 'Why should it matter how long I've known? You've deceived me from the beginning, when you introduced yourself as Charles Richards. Why, Charles? *Why?*'

'*Stalemate,*' he said with a ferocious smile. '*You tell me why I can't go home with you and I'll tell you why I didn't give you my real name.*'

'Stalemate, indeed,' she answered as evenly as she could.

'Don't you recognise the name?'

She would swear he hadn't meant to ask that question. 'No. Should I?'

He answered with a question of his own, his voice raw with suppressed emotion. 'So what are we going to do now? Kiss each other goodbye and say thanks for the nice affair?'

'I said I'd call you tomorrow.'

He dropped her arm. 'Was it that for you, Laura? A pleasant summer love affair, a passing interlude you'll remember with a smile and then eventually forget?'

What was she supposed to say? I love you, body and soul, in a way I never loved Bart. I'll never forget you ... With a forced smile she said, 'How can I answer that now? You'd better ask me again in six months' time.'

'I have to go back to Toronto in September.'

Stalemate. Impasse. What did it matter which word they used? It was an ending full of ambiguity, a goodbye fraught with fear. Her face tight with strain, Laura said, 'Charles, I've got to go—I'm worried about Darren. I'd really appreciate it if you'd make sure the cottage is left as I found it ... Jane's sister is supposed to be here for most of August.' She produced the faintest of smiles. 'And I'd also appreciate it if you'd help me carry out my suitcases. I seem to have an awful lot of stuff.'

Without a word he bent and picked up the nearest case. She took one last look around the cottage, trying to ignore the bedroom where she and Charles had shared such happiness, recognising the one thing she had not dared to ask him. She could have thrown his own question back at him. *Was it a passing interlude for you, Charles?* But she had not dared to do so. Was she a coward? Or was she simply protecting herself from knowledge too painful to bear?

It took only a few minutes to load all her belongings

in the boot of her car. Charles slammed the bootlid shut
and passed her the keys. Every nerve ending she
possessed screaming with tension, Laura took them
from him, trying not to touch him. Moving towards the
driver's door, she said, 'I promise I'll call you
tomorrow.' But before she could get in, he had put a
hand on her shoulder. She turned her head, felt her
heart melt at the look in his eyes and then was locked in
his arms. In one kiss he expressed with passion and
anger all the joy of their lovemaking and the pain of
their parting.

She was shaking when he released her, and bereft of
speech. Fumbling with the door handle, she got in the
car. Charles shut the door. She started the engine,
backed up and drove away. She did not look back.

CHAPTER TEN

IT was nearly midnight when Laura drove into Grantham. Although coffee and her own thoughts had kept her awake, she was conscious of a deep inner tiredness, pervasive enough that for a moment she debated whether she should drive straight home and simply 'phone the hospital for a report on Darren's progress; she could see him tomorrow when she was feeling stronger.

Conscience or stubbornness prevented her from following this easy path. She drove past the house, noticing the lights still burning on the porch and in the kitchen, and three blocks further on turned left into the hospital parking lot, where she parked the car and went in the main door. Visiting hours were long past, but the staff knew Laura and in a few minutes she was talking to the nurse who was in charge of the men's surgical ward and who was a friend of Jane's. 'Darren's fine. No complications and he's strong as an ox, should recover in no time. Want to see him? I have to check his blood pressure anyway.'

There were two other men in the ward, both older than Darren. That was what struck Laura: how young Darren looked and how vulnerable, with his dark lashes sweeping his cheeks and his mouth relaxed in sleep.

As the nurse wrapped the pressure sleeve around his arm, his lashes quivered and his eyes opened. He blinked a few times, fighting against the drugs he had been given for the pain, obviously trying to get his bearings. The nurse let the air out of the sleeve, wrote the numbers down in her notebook and said, 'Someone here to see you, Darren.' To Laura she added placidly, 'Don't stay too long, dear, the supervisor would have my head if she knew you were here.'

'I won't.' Laura turned back to Darren, who was watching her with a puzzled frown on his face. In the four years she had known him she had never got close to Darren, for he had rebuffed her at every turn; yet as she saw him lying there in the narrow hospital bed she felt a surge of love for him mingled with a heartfelt gratitude that he was alive and recovering. Tears blurred her eyes, for it had been a long day. Impulsively she bent and kissed his cheek, feeling the roughness of his beard against her lips. 'I'm so glad you're all right,' she whispered.

He was still frowning. 'Did you drive from Cape Breton?' he muttered.

'Yes. Keith called me this afternoon and I left right away.' After a fight with Charles.

'But you're still on holiday.'

She had no idea whether he was pleased to see her or angry that she had come. She thought of saying, 'Oh well, I was ready to come home anyway,' then discarded it for the truth. 'I had to come. I was worried about you.'

The pupils of his eyes were dilated and he was struggling for words. 'I knew you'd come for Sue-Ann or Keith. I didn't think you would for me.'

When she took his hand, the one without the intravenous, his fingers lay limply in hers. 'Of course I would,' she said as strongly as she could; and because it was midnight and he was drugged and she was exhausted, she said, 'I love you, Darren. Of course I'd come when you're ill.'

She felt his fingers move in her grasp as tentatively as the first movements of a newborn animal. But the drugs were clouding his brain. 'Afraid . . . I'll lose my job,' he faltered. 'Will you go . . . see them, Laura?'

She pressed his hand. 'Sure I will. First thing tomorrow morning.'

'Thanks.' As his lashes drooped to his cheeks, he gave a vague smile in her direction. 'Thanks, Laura . . . glad you came.'

She had not imagined those last three words, spoken so quietly that she had had to strain to hear them. From Darren they were a huge admission. Unashamedly Laura let the tears trickle down her cheeks, stroking the hardness of his calloused palm as his breathing deepened to the rhythms of sleep. She thought of her brother, James, who had belittled his elder son in favour of his second child, brilliant, fine-tuned Keith, and knew she had reaped the bitter harvest of James's insensitivity. Of course Darren had rejected her. Rejected himself, he had fought back the only way he knew how. But tonight had provided a break in the self-defeating pattern of their relationship. A small break. But a break, nevertheless, and one which Laura felt in a surge of optimism would survive the rigours of morning.

Very gently she released Darren's hand and crept out of the ward, waving at Jane's friend, who was busy at the other end of the corridor. The night air was cool and damp. She took a couple of deep breaths, noticing the absolute stillness of the elm trees and the darkness of the houses: the inhabitants of Grantham were in bed, as all decent people should be at this hour. Four years she had spent in this town, and would spend one more. Standing quietly beside her car she began to understand how deeply those four years had affected her, with all their ups and downs, all the crises and joys of shepherding three young people towards independence and maturity. At times she had railed against the fate that had brought her to this sleepy little town so far from the city and the studies that she loved. Now she realised, humbly, that she would be a much better doctor because of her years of surrogate parenthood, kinder, more tolerant, less impatient. Slowly she drove home.

Keith was still up, sitting with his feet on the kitchen table reading the newspaper and drinking strong black tea, the overhead light turning his hair to flame; as she opened the back door and saw him Laura was reminded of Annie's equally startling, if artificially produced, coiffure. When he heard her come in, Keith dropped the paper and his feet to the floor. 'Laura! I was beginning to wonder if I should send out a search party.' He gave her a bone-cracking hug, then peered down at her face. 'Hey—are you okay?'

She managed a watery smile. 'Darren was pleased to see me. I know he was pleased. I—I guess that really got to me.' In a rush she added, 'I'm so glad I've had the chance to be with the three of you since your father died, Keith, I've learned such a lot that I'd never have learned out of medical texts.'

Keith put his arms around her again, pressing her tear-wet face to his shoulder. 'Darling Laura . . . you've been good for us as well. All three of us. I've seen Darren watching you, trying to figure you out. He was too stiff-necked to change his behaviour—but I'm sure there were times he wanted to. And Sue-Ann would have been lost without you. She's really missed you the last three weeks.'

'And you, Keith? What about you?' Laura was not fishing for compliments; she really wanted to know.

'Oh, that's easy. Apart from making a home out of a house and giving us the routine and security we needed—no small accomplishment, I'll never knock women who choose to stay home with their families and do just that—you've given me a fabulous role-model: someone who knows what she wants and will work like crazy to get it. It's partly because of you that I got up the nerve to apply for those auditions.'

'Oh.' She rubbed at her eyes, which were full of tears again. 'But I didn't *do* anything, Keith.'

'You were just yourself. And now I'm going to pack you off to bed, you look half dead. Leave me your keys, I'll bring all your stuff in. Sue-Ann's feeling better, by the way. I think she lost everything there was to lose, poor kid.'

Her voice muffled in his sweater, Laura said, 'Oh, Keith, it's nice to be home.'

'Nice to have you home,' he said briskly, obviously deciding there had been enough emotion for one evening. 'Off you go.'

'Wake me up before you go to work, will you? I told Darren I'd go over to the dairy farm, he's afraid of losing his job.'

'He sure likes that place. I've got the morning off, but I'll get you up around nine, how's that? Go to bed, Laura.'

Her smile was more convincing. 'Yessir . . . thanks, Keith.'

She trailed up the stairs and peeked into Sue-Ann's room, which looked as if it had not been tidied since Laura had left. Sue-Ann was curled up in the middle of the bed, fast asleep. Despite Darren's gibes she still slept with a huge and somewhat battered teddy bear at the foot of her bed, and again Laura felt that treacherous lump in her throat.

Softly she closed Sue-Ann's door, went to her own room, undressed and tumbled into bed. Charles, in whose arms she had slept the night before, seemed a very long way away; closing her mind against the pain of memory Laura fell asleep.

The birds were silent. She must have slept in.

Laura heard a tap at her door, muttered into the pillow, 'Charles?' then hurriedly sat up. She wasn't at the cottage. She was home. She said loudly, 'Keith?' and hoped he had not heard her all-revealing use of another man's name as she woke up.

'Eight-thirty, Laura. Coffee's made.'

'I'll be right down—thanks.'

Her cases, she saw, were lined up at the foot of her bed. She padded to the window and drew the curtains.

Her room was at the back of the house. The orchard stretched in straight rows down the slope; the apples, naturally enough, had grown larger while she was away, and she could smell the newly mown grass. She was home. She closed her eyes and hugged her body, remembering Charles, wondering if she would ever feel truly at home without him. She had to 'phone him later on this morning, although she had no idea what she was going to say.

Not bothering to unpack anything but the essentials, Laura showered and dressed in a red denim jumpsuit, an outfit Charles had not seen and which consequently carried with it no memories. Then she ran downstairs. Keith's coffee was as strong as the tea he brewed; she added lots of cream and sugar, thought of Charles's three teaspoonfuls and said brightly, 'Want some more toast?'

Keith patted his lean belly. 'No, thanks. Don't want to get fat. Sue-Ann's still asleep, isn't she?'

'Yes. I thought I'd leave her. I'll run over to the farm and go to the hospital, and see her when I get back.' She buttered her toast and added some of her own homemade strawberry jam. 'Tell me how to get to the farm.'

The dairy farm was at the base of South Mountain. Mixed herds of Holsteins and Guernseys were grazing in the lush green meadows, while heifers bawled from one of the barns. Laura found the owner of the farm, Pieter VanZoost, a big, slow-moving Dutchman, tinkering with a tractor parked in one of the sheds. Her eyes adjusting to the shade, she said tentatively, 'Mr VanZoost?' hoping she had pronounced his name correctly.

He put down a wrench and wiped his hands on a piece of rag. '*Ja?*'

'I'm Darren Walker's aunt—Laura Walker.'

'His aunt?' A benign smile spread across his face. 'You look more like his sister.'

She side-stepped this remark with all its attendant explanations. 'Darren asked me to come and see you. He's worried about his job.'

'Worried? But I 'phoned the hospital and they said he would be soon home.'

'He will be. But he won't be able to do heavy physical work for several weeks.'

'*Ja*, that I understand.' Pieter VanZoost gave her another benign smile.

He was very much like the teddy bear that sat on Sue-Ann's bed, Laura decided. 'Darren's afraid you'll have to get someone else in his place.'

'Two of my sons and a neighbour's boy will do the extra work while school is out. By September Darren will be back, isn't it so?'

'I would think so. You mean you'll keep him on?'

'That is what I say to you,' Pieter VanZoost remarked patiently. 'He is very good with animals—the cows and the heifers—and he works hard and learns fast. I wait for him to come back, *ja*.'

Her smile was brilliant. 'Thank you, he'll be so glad to hear that. I know he likes the job.'

'Then we are all happy,' said the farmer, picking up the wrench again. 'Tell him to come anytime for a visit.'

Having said goodbye, Laura walked out of the shed and along the grassy track between the barns. The air was pungent with the small of manure. Rather Darren than her. But the outbuildings were well-maintained and the cows had a sleek glossiness to their flanks, which even she, an amateur, could appreciate. Her face very thoughtful, she drove to the hospital.

Darren was sitting up in bed. He looked pale and heavy-eyed, regarding her with a wariness that inwardly she could only reciprocate, for she had no idea whether he would remember their midnight conversation.

'Hello, Darren,' she said, trying to convey the right degree of sympathy without any over-solicitude. 'Hurting?'

'Yeah. Don't know which is worse, the pain or the drugs. One hurts, the other makes me feel punch-drunk. Did you go to the farm?'

So he remembered that much . . . 'Yes. He's expecting you back in September and his sons will pick up the slack in the meantime. He says you're good with animals, you work hard and you learn fast.'

Darren came as near to blushing as he ever would 'Oh. Good.'

'The cows, presumably, miss you, too,' she added mischievously.

'Shove it, Laura,' he growled. But it was such a good-natured growl that she knew he remembered everything that had been said at midnight.

She leaned forward. 'Darren, one of the things I did while I was away was to plan some sort of financial strategy. I've put aside money for Sue-Ann's nursing and Keith's singing lessons and of course an equal amount for you. Maybe eventually you might want to set up your own dairy operation.'

'There's some land for sale not far from Pieter's.'

'So you'd already thought of it.'

'Although I want to go to agricultural college first. Don't know which is best—to learn from books or on the job. Never did have much use for books, did I?'

'You were never encouraged to, Darren.'

He looked her in the eye, and between them lay James, who had always dismissed Darren as the stupid one of the family. 'Guess you're right.'

'I know I'm right. Anyway, I just want you to know that the money's available.'

'Thanks, Laura.' He was smoothing the hem of the sheet. 'I wasn't very nice to you about that money.'

'I didn't know how to handle it, either. In some ways I still don't.' She hadn't trusted Charles enough to reveal to him that she was a rich woman; she had assumed he was like Bart, to whom her money was lure enough to marry her. 'But if I spread the money around I can do a lot with it,' she went on. 'And it will be wonderful not to have to worry about all the expenses of medical school ... Darren, you look tired. Do you want me to put the bed down so you can rest?'

That he did not argue was an admission of his level of discomfort. She lowered the head of the bed and straightened his pillows. Then, almost shyly, she kissed his cheek, noticing that someone had shaved him this morning. 'I'll drop in later on.'

Awkwardly, because he still had an intravenous drip, he raised his hand in salute as she left the room. She would get no flowery speeches from Darren, nor could he emulate Keith's quicksilver sensitivity or Sue-Ann's warm-hearted affection. By nature he was reserved, not to say dour. But Laura knew the last twelve hours had marked a change for the better in their relationship, an easing of his resentment, a lessening of her defences; and with that she was satisfied.

She drove home slowly down the three-shaded main street, waving at familiar faces and noticing all the old landmarks: the pharmacy owned by Jane's husband, the post office, the bank and the church—whose steeple still needed painting. She saw Mrs Manning talking earnestly to two other women and wondered if she, Laura, who had refused to marry Bart, was the subject of the discussion. It was not unlikely.

She turned into the driveway and parked the car, enjoying the sun on her face. She still felt a little ashamed of the whole Bart episode. Perhaps he had been a necessary part of her growing up, and certainly he had made her understand how propinquity and loneliness could breed emotions that might be mistaken for love. It had taken Charles to show her how far astray she had drifted. She loved Charles. Whether she would ever have the chance to tell him so was another question . . .

With an impatient sigh she got out of the car and ran into the house. Sue-Ann was sitting at the kitchen table in a pretty flowered négligé, looking interestingly pale, while Keith, wrapped in a bright red apron that clashed with his hair, was busy at the stove. When she saw Laura, Sue-Ann leaped up and flung her arms around her aunt. 'I'm *so* glad to see you!' she cried, a break in her voice.

'She doesn't like my cooking,' said Keith, sprinkling herbs into the eggs he was scrambling.

Sue-Ann giggled. 'I got sick the day after eating a dinner he'd cooked. Pure coincidence, of course,' she added hastily, as Keith brandished the wooden spoon at her. With considerable dignity she sat down at the table again. 'I keep hoping he'll make me a decent cup of tea—not that black brew he puts on the back burner and boils for half an hour.'

'See what I've had to put up with, Laura?' Keith said cheerfully. 'Do you think I should add a touch of oregano?'

Sue-Ann gave a histrionic shudder. 'How about some chilli powder?'

Laura began to laugh. 'Stop it, you two! I'm beginning to feel as if I've never been away. I'll make you a cup of tea, Sue-Ann. Tell me about your love life.'

Steven, it appeared, was an amalgam of every possible virtue, not the least of which was that he was as much enraptured by Sue-Ann as she by him. 'He's such a hunk,' said Sue-Ann dreamily. 'I'm really in love this time, Laura.'

Laura merely smiled, having heard this sentiment expressed before, and put a mug of weak tea in front of her niece. 'A piece of toast? You should probably eat something.'

'I guess I could manage a piece of toast. Amazing—I do feel a bit hungry today. Yesterday I couldn't even look a glass of ginger ale in the eye.'

'I didn't sing a note all day,' said Keith nobly. 'I hope you appreciate that, sis.'

'Oh, I do. I——'

Someone knocked at the back door. Laura, who was taking a couple of slices of bread out of the bag, had time to think, *I hope that's not Bart*, before Keith said, 'I'll get it.'

He went to the door. As a deep voice said, 'Do I have the right house for Laura Walker?' Laura dropped the bag of bread on the floor. It was not Bart.

She clutched the edge of the counter, thinking with great clarity, I am not going to faint. That would be a ridiculous thing to do. Dreadfully Victorian.

Keith said unnecessarily, 'Someone here to see you, Laura.'

She let go of the counter. 'Hello, Charles,' she said. He was wearing crumpled cords and a T-shirt, was unshaven, and looked as if he had not slept all night. Somehow he had run her to ground. He was here in Grantham, where everyone knew her as the winner of the lottery. She said with intentional rudeness and a complete lack of welcome, 'What are you doing here?'

'Hoping you'll offer me a cup of tea ... and introduce me to these people.' He indicated Sue-Ann and Keith, who were staring at him in fascination.

Her piose appeared to have vanished along with her good manners. Laura took a deep breath and said levelly, 'My niece Sue-Ann and my nephew Keith. This is Charles Thorndyke.' She emphasised the surname very slightly, knowing only Charles would realise the significance of this.

Keith, who had the assurance to carry off any number of red aprons, said politely, 'How do you do?' and gave the eggs another stir.

Sue-Ann said artlessly, 'Are you the man from the next-door cottage?'

Laura raised her eyes to heaven. 'Yes, he is the man from the next-door cottage. What I would like to know is what he's doing here.'

Hurriedly Sue-Ann interposed, 'You dropped the bread, Laura. Why don't you pick it up while I pour him a cup of tea? Then Keith and I will eat our breakfast in the dining room, won't we, Keith?'

Charles said grimly, 'I've got a better idea.' He marched across the room, spun Laura around and kissed her hard on the mouth.

She kicked out at him and felt her foot sink into the loaf of bread. Behind them Keith burst into the magnificent aria *Celeste Aida*, gesturing with the wooden spoon. The effect on Charles was electrifying. He dropped Laura's shoulders and said, 'Good God!'

Laura was more used to Keith's glorious voice and to his habit of singing around the house. 'Shut up, Keith,' she said crossly. But Charles gave her a shake and obligingly Keith completed the aria, sketching a bow with the wooden spoon held to his heart. Sue-Ann took one look at Laura's face, grabbed Keith and the saucepan of eggs and shepherded them both out of the kitchen, closing the door behind her.

Laura bent down and picked up the mutilated bag of bread. Slapping it on the counter, she stamped her foot in an intoxicating burst of temper. '*Why* did you have to come here?' she cried.

'I wanted to find out what you were hiding ... I thought you might have a stray husband or two lying around, or a bevy of crazy aunts.' Appreciatively he looked around the pleasant, sunlit kitchen. 'No signs of either one. Should I check the attics?'

She was not in the mood to be laughed at. 'I think you should go back where you came from and wait for a proper invitation.'

'I might have to wait for a very long time.' With an air of being very much at home, Charles hooked one of the kitchen chairs with his foot and sat down. 'How about that cup of tea, I've had a long drive. I like Sue-Ann and Keith, by the way. What an incredible voice he has. I can see why Besicaglia is interested.'

Laura put a mug of tea in front of Charles, saw his lean, well-kept hands curve around it, thought of them on her body and said in a strangled voice, 'Do you want a piece of toast?'

'That would be nice, thank you.'

She pushed the lever on the toaster. 'Don't be so bloody polite,' she grated. 'How did you find me? I never told you where I lived.'

'You didn't, did you?' He was stirring sugar into his tea. 'After you left yesterday, I debated following you— one way to find out where you live. However, I figured you might not like that. So I got up very early this morning, drove to Halifax, went to a library and went through the 'phone books for the Annapolis Valley until I found your name. Main Street, Grantham. Easy.'

She was impressed in spite of herself. 'How did you know which house was ours?'

'I stopped at the gas station down the road and asked the guy on the pumps.'

'And what did he say?'

'He said it was a grand day, wasn't it, although we could do with a mite of rain. And the Walker house is the fifth one on the right past King Street.'

'And that's all?'

He was watching the play of expression on her face. 'That's all, and no, I didn't talk to anyone else. What are you so afraid that I'll hear, Laura?'

The toast popped up, she buttered it, put it on a plate and passed him a knife, a serviette and the jam. Then she poured herself a cup of tea, all without saying a word.

Charles spread jam on the one corner of the toast. 'I don't know what you're afraid of. But I do know this—I cannot believe you've done anything wrong, or that there's some kind of secret in your past that you're ashamed of. Oddly enough, because you've been no more honest with me in one respect that I've been with you, I'd stake my life on your integrity, Laura. I've grown to know a warm, responsive, generous woman. I don't think you need hide anything from me.'

Laura suddenly felt like crying. Charles had put into words his testament of faith in her, and she knew she would treasure those words as long as she lived. She had once said to him that she wanted him to think well of her. She need never doubt that he did.

She raised her head, finally allowing her emotion to show. 'Oh Charles . . . it's strange you should say that, because I've had exactly the same feelings about you. Yet I couldn't understand why you should keep your real name hidden from me.'

'You've never heard the name Thorndyke?'

'No.'

'That puts me in my place.' He got up from the table, going to stand by the window that overlooked the peaceful, leafy tunnels of the orchard. 'When I said I came here to find out what you were hiding, that was the truth. But only part of the truth.' As he paused, the tension in his posture communicated itself to Laura, so that she braced herself for whatever was to come. 'I came to tell you something,' he went on. 'Something I've been aware of for some time more or less subconsciously, but which hit me like a ton of bricks when you drove away yesterday evening. I've fallen in love with you, Laura. I want to marry you.'

From upstairs floated an echo of *Celeste Aida*. Keith was singing again. 'You love *me*?' Laura repeated incredulously.

'That's what I said.'

'Ordinary Laura Walker?'

'Bright, dedicated, responsible, fun-loving, fiery-tempered, passionate Laura Walker,' Charles responded promptly, his eyes on the wonder in her face. 'Scarcely ordinary.'

'But you love me for myself.'

'How else could I love you, Laura?'

She got up, standing uncertainly by the table. 'Charles, I've got something to confess. I've got a million dollars.'

Whatever reply he had been expecting to his avowal of love, it was obviously not the one he had been given. He looked at her as if she were crazy. 'What on earth are you talking about?'

'I'm rich,' she said apologetically. 'A couple of

months ago I won the lottery—one million dollars. That's what I've been hiding. That's why I didn't want you to come to Grantham, because everyone here knows about it. I was the talk of the town.'

'Let me get this straight,' Charles said. 'You didn't want me to know that you have a million dollars. Why not?'

'That's why Bart proposed to me,' she said obliquely.

'So?'

'So I wanted you to be different. If you were to propose to me, it would be because you wanted *me*. Not my money.'

'And if I were to propose to you—wanting you and not your money—what were you planning to reply, ordinary Laura Walker?'

Her smile was radiant, her bearing suddenly full of confidence. 'Why, I would say yes, please, I'd love to marry you.'

His eyes shone with the flash of light on steel. 'And why would you love to marry me?'

'Because I love you, Charles Richard Thorndyke, whoever-you-are.'

'And what if I told you I was a pauper without two cents to rub together?'

'A million dollars should be plenty for both of us. Even if I do paint the church steeple.'

'But what if I told you my father is one of the twenty richest men in Canada?'

He was deadly serious; the flip reply that had been on the tip of her tongue fled. She said slowly, 'You mean it.'

'Yes. David Richard Thorndyke, self-made millionaire, president of a dozen companies, on the board of a dozen more, as autocratic a man as ever lived. My father.'

'So my million dollars doesn't matter?'

'No. I'm an only child and my father's heir. I certainly don't need it. You'll never have to worry that I'm after your money, Laura.'

She was beginning to understand a great deal. She said astutely, 'But you were afraid I might be after yours.'

'The more I got to know you the less likely that seemed. But for once in my life I wanted to be loved for myself. In the group I moved with in Ontario I was a marked man, heir to a fortune, women falling all over me. Me and my wallet, that is. But at the cottage I was Charles Richards, who was rapidly falling in love with Laura Walker.'

'So *you* didn't want me to find out about your money and *I* didn't want you to find out about mine. Charles, what fools we've been!'

'Not really. You don't know how badly I wanted you to care for *me*. Me alone. Not the heir to the Thorndyke fortune. The more deeply I fell in love with you, the more important that became—and the more afraid I grew of whatever it was you were hiding.'

Laura had had enough of words. 'Charles, kiss me,' she said.

She closed her eyes and tilted her face, and heard his exultant laugh. 'Delighted to oblige.'

They kissed for a long time, kisses of passion and laughter and discovery; and in between, in broken phrases they began learning the ardent, intensely private language of new lovers. The things they said Laura never shared with anyone; they were to remain always with her, glowing like precious jewels in the quiet places of her soul.

In a crescendo of sound, singing scales, Keith approached the kitchen door. He ended on middle C and said tactfully, 'Excuse me, Laura—are you still there?'

Blushing, Laura removed one hand from Charles's hair and the other from under his shirt where it had been caressing the muscled flatness of his belly. Charles slid his palms from her breasts to the curve of her waist. Holding her close he said, 'You're safe to come in, Keith.'

Holding the red apron and the saucepan, now empty of scrambled eggs, Keith sidled round the door. He raised an expressive eyebrow when he saw the pair of them locked in each other's arms and called over his shoulder, 'You win, Sue-Ann.' To Laura and Charles he added, 'She thinks you're in love.'

'Clever girl,' said Charles. 'Your aunt is going to marry me.'

Sue-Ann had been creeping along the hall behind Keith. When she heard Charles she gave a shriek of delight and flung herself at the two of them, hugging them indiscriminately. 'I'm so happy for you! Laura, can I be a bridesmaid? I'm glad you're not marrying Bart, I was afraid you might.' Her vivid little face laughed up at Charles. 'You're a hunk.'

'That's high praise,' Laura commented drily.

Keith, more on his dignity, shook Charles's hand, said warmly, 'Congratulations,' and kissed Laura with equal warmth.

Sue-Ann believed in getting to the essentials. 'When's the wedding?'

Charles smiled at Laura. 'We hadn't got around to that. I think it should be this autumn, sweetheart, before I go to Toronto. If I'm going to be flying here every weekend we'd better be legally married—or else the neighbours will talk. What do you think?'

'You mean you're marrying me because of the neighbours?'

'You know damn well why I'm marrying you,' he said roughly. 'Because I love you to distraction and can't live without you.' Then he caught sight of Sue-Ann's wide, entranced eyes, and helplessly began to laugh. 'And we'll have the sweetest bridesmaid this side of the Rockies, don't you agree?'

'Definitely!' Laura said. 'September's a lovely month for a wedding. Keith can sing, and Darren—why,

Darren can give me away.'

'Would he do that?' Keith asked doubtfully.

'Yes,' she answered slowly, 'yes, I think he would. Charles, we must go to the hospital this afternoon, I want you to meet him.'

'In the meantime I'm going to the liquor store to get a bottle of champagne,' Keith said decisively. 'Salami sandwiches and champagne for lunch.'

'And I'll go upstairs and get dressed,' Sue-Ann added. She smiled kindly at Laura and Charles, said, 'You'll be quite safe for half an hour,' and fled, laughing, before Laura could retaliate.

The kitchen was empty but for the two of them. Charles said a little dazedly, 'A ready-made family.'

'Do you mind?'

'Mind? I love it. I was an only child, remember?'

'Whose mother always bought expensive birthday cakes.'

'Yeah ... and whose father was always too busy making money to bother with birthdays at all. You've probably realised by now that the 'phone call you overheard at the cottage was from my father. I was afraid you'd caught the beginning of the call when I asked for him by name, and that you'd connect the name with the sums of money we'd been mentioning and figure out who I was. At that point I wanted to be Charles Richards, not Charles Thorndyke.'

'Which is why you were so angry.'

There was a long silence while Charles made a belated apology. Then he said, his arms still around Laura, 'Dad and I rarely see eye-to-eye, I'd better warn you about that now. After I finished university, I worked for him for three years, long enough to know we operate on two different wavelengths. We had some stupendous fights when I started freelancing, and eventually I took off around the world for a couple of years. Took five hundred dollars with me and worked my way from place to place. Arrived home with two hundred and thirty-six dollars and fifteen cents. I had to do that, Laura. I had to prove to myself that I could exist without my father's money. I've been taking this summer at the cottage, which incidentally belongs to a distant cousin of my mother's, to consolidate all I've learned. I'm going back to Toronto in the atumn. But on my terms.'

Laure had the feeling he was condensing a great many experiences into very few words; but, she thought with a catch of pure happiness, she would have all the time in the world to learn the details. 'And what are your terms?'

'In Scots Bay I started a basketball team with a bunch of kids who were hanging around the streets,' he replied. 'If you built a gymnasium and hired some instructors you could do wonders there . . . I guess what I want to do is start with my father's various concerns, factories, mines and so on, and see what could be done to improve the leisure hours and the working conditions of his employees. Take my time and study each situation, spend the money wisely— but spend it. I have the feeling in the long run productivity would increase—an argument that will convince my father.'

'I think you'd do well at that,' she said sincerely, remembering his rapport with the basketball team: Charles cared about people and was not afraid to translate that caring into concrete action. 'But Charles, if I'm at medical school in Toronto and you're travelling all around the country, will our marriage do well?'

'Yes,' he said firmly. 'We'll buy a house in Toronto as close to the university as possible, that'll be a start. I'm sure we'll have to work a little harder than most couples to get time together, but the time we do have will be quality time and we'll take full advantage of it.' He looked at his watch. 'For instance, we've got a few minutes alone in the kitchen before Sue-Ann arrives to talk about bridesmaid's dresses and Keith arrives to get us drunk on champagne. Let me show you how we can take advantage of it.'

And he did so, in a manner very satisfactory to both of them.

Harlequin Presents

Coming Next Month

911 TO FILL A SILENCE Jayne Bauling
Bustling Taipei sets the scene for a reunion between a free-lance radio
reporter and her celebrated ex-husband. He's still as charming and
impulsive as ever—the sort of man who'd marry on a whim.

912 TITAN'S WOMAN Ann Charlton
When a powerful Australian developer gives in to a woman's concern for
the environment, the newspapers dub them "TITAN and the Amazon."
Then he, an experienced infighter, goes straight for the heart!

913 HUNTER'S PREY Jasmine Cresswell
For two years a runaway wife has fled from city to city, state to state, to
hide herself and her child from the only man she's ever loved. And now
he's found her....

914 WHAT'S RIGHT Melinda Cross
A powerful force draws an interior designer to a wealthy American
businessman, though a tragic sense of loyalty binds him to another. But
his determination to do what's right only makes her love him more.

915 CHANCE MEETINGS Vanessa James
A man—a rich man—is needed to save her family's Cornish estate. And
just like that, two marriageable men happen along—one for Caro and one
for her cousin. But nothing's so easy....

916 FIRE WITH FIRE Penny Jordan
When a London newscaster sacrifices everything but her ethics to repay
a wily entrepreneur for her sister's recklessness, it occurs to him that he
could use a woman like her in his life.

917 A RISKY BUSINESS Sandra K. Rhoades
Risks come with the territory for an Alberta oil scout. But she doesn't
plan to risk her heart—not until she's caught snooping around a self-
made millionaire's oilfields.

918 LIKE ENEMIES Sophie Weston
With ten-year-old headlines of the family scandal still etched in her mind,
a London designer is frightened and confused by her feelings for an
alluring international businessman.

Available in September wherever paperback books are sold, or through
Harlequin Reader Service:

In the U.S.
P.O. Box 1397
Buffalo, N.Y.
14240-1397

In Canada
P.O. Box 2800, Postal Station A
5170 Yonge Street
Willowdale, Ontario M2N 6J3

Could she find love as a mail-order bride?

MARIANNE WILLMAN

PIECES OF SKY

In the Arizona of 1873, Nora O'Shea is caught between life with a contemptuous, arrogant husband and her desperate love for Roger LeBeau, half-breed Comanche Indian scout and secret freedom fighter.

———————•———————

Take 4 books & a surprise gift FREE

SPECIAL LIMITED-TIME OFFER

Mail to   **Harlequin Reader Service**®

In the U.S.	In Canada
901 Fuhrmann Blvd.	P.O. Box 2800, Station "A"
P.O. Box 1394	5170 Yonge Street
Buffalo, N.Y. 14240-1394	Willowdale, Ontario M2N 6J3

YES! Please send me 4 free Harlequin Romance® novels and my free surprise gift. Then send me 6 brand-new novels every month as they come off the presses. Bill me at the low price of $1.65 each ($1.75 in Canada)—a 11% saving off the retail price. There are no shipping, handling or other hidden costs. There is no minimum number of books I must purchase. I can always return a shipment and cancel at any time. Even if I never buy another book from Harlequin, the 4 free novels and the surprise gift are mine to keep forever.   106-BPP-BP6F

Name   (PLEASE PRINT)

Address   Apt. No.

City   State/Prov.   Zip/Postal Code

This offer is limited to one order per household and not valid to present subscribers. Price is subject to change.   DOR-SUB-1R

ATTRACTIVE, SPACE SAVING BOOK RACK

Display your most prized novels on this handsome and sturdy book rack. The hand-rubbed walnut finish will blend into your library decor with quiet elegance, providing a practical organizer for your favorite hard-or softcovered books.

Only $9.95

*Approximately
16" x 8"
when assembled*

Assembles in seconds!

To order, rush your name, address and zip code, along with a check or money order for $10.70 ($9.95 plus 75¢ postage and handling) (New York residents add appropriate sales tax), payable to *Harlequin Reader Service* to:

In the U.S.

Harlequin Reader Service
Book Rack Offer
901 Fuhrmann Blvd.
P.O. Box 1325
Buffalo, NY 14269-1325

Offer not available in Canada.

BKR–1